# MW's 1

## Fiction short stories

# THE FENNIGAN CASE

## The Plea

*"I can't find the staircase!"*

"That's the last we heard from Andy Wallace and Chuck Robbins, our TV crew, about fifteen hours ago. We are not sure at this point what happened out there. Please … please, if anyone has any information we would appreciate it if you'd give us a call at the phone number at the bottom of your screen…"

Jim Colby talked to the camera, feeling chills running down his spine.

He had been in the news business for over forty-two years but had never seen anything like this. He felt guilty; it somehow was his fault.

He should have known better.

Nothing made sense. Nothing.

He felt tired; after being in the newsroom for over thirty-six straight hours, he started feeling very tired, and now wanted to push everything away from his mind.

His coworkers advised him to go home.

Andy's girlfriend, Amanda, kept calling every hour, to see if there was any news. Very soon she would be on her way to the TV station, and Jim would have some serious explaining to do.

Should he show her the tape?

Should he show Andy's last broadcast to her?

No. It would be better not to show it to anyone just yet. A few people had seen it already and they were still deeply disturbed by it; it would be better to wait for the outcome, before showing it to anyone. E

Especially someone close to his missing crew.

Jim left his office, and the tape was concealed in his firm grasp, under his jacket. He had to take it to a safe place; he knew just the right person to take it to, but Jim was not quite sure how to proceed after that.

Marla approached him as he left.

"Mr. Colby! Please … there are two police officers on their way over here to talk to you. It's important … they said … Where are you going? Can I call your cell? Sir?"

"Call my cell; that's fine. Tell whoever is looking for me that you don't know where I went. Just take messages, Marla."

He drove home -or so he thought.

He needed to drive, go elsewhere; clear his mind, if such a thing was even possible, at all.

He had to try.

After a while, he stopped at Joe's Bar, and although it was 11:30 in the morning, he thought he could use a drink.

To hell with AA for today; he just needed to make sense out of the last forty hours, somehow.

Besides, he couldn't go home to Marjorie, not in that state of mind.

She probably saw the broadcast and by now, she sure would be very worried; just like everyone else.

"Hey, Jimmy… Coffee?" Joe asked as he greeted Jim.

"Nah, bourbon with ice… And make it double," James replied as he sat on a stool, by the counter.

"Whoa, Jim! You haven't drunk in over twelve years now…"

"It's okay, Joe…. I really need it. It all can go to hell, just for today. I really don't care."

"I see. Rough night last night, huh? I saw the evening news … well, you know, everyone saw it … so … er … what happened back there, Jim? Not that I'm curious, but people have been talking about that since last night … and … how are Andy and Chuck doing? Was that a publicity stunt of sorts?"

Jim drank the last drop of that bourbon in one big swallow. He sighed before answering.

"How many years have I been in this business Joe? Tell me."

"Well … uh … I'm not sure. Ever since I've known you; that's for sure. Why do you ask? Is everything okay?"

A long silence followed, and Jim Colby gestured at Joe to pour some more bourbon in his empty glass, where two lonely ice cubes stood - one on top of the other.

Jim looked around Joe's Bar, as his friend poured him another drink.

It was right there, at that bar, that Jim had first interviewed Andy - only six months ago, Jim thought.

Only six months ago Andy seemed like the perfect candidate Jim needed for the new Special Reports segment; Jim also remembered that although he was not impressed with Andy's resume and previous work experience, he'd make sure to give the boy a hard time.

After all, it was Andy's first 'real' job, outside college.

Jim thought if the boy really wanted to do something in the KLT TV station, he'd have to put up with a few things.

Jim sighed and turned to speak to Joe, "Almost forty-three years, Joe; forty-three damn years in this business and I feel I haven't learned a thing. I started off selling newspapers on a corner stand in Chicago, when I was fifteen … I can say I am a self-made man, Joe. Someone like you, tenacious to the core, never one to give up on things … and now, well, I'll be damned, but I have been thinking about resigning for the past three hours… This is the end for me, Joe. I can't go on anymore, not after what happened last night..."

Jim Colby's cell went off.

He almost spilled the second, untouched drink on the counter while hurrying to get his phone out of his jacket's inside pocket.

"Colby," he answered it, shaking a little bit.

After a couple of seconds he said, "Yeah, I know. Well, what the hell do you want me to do? No, I don't have the damn tape! But if I did, I wouldn't let anyone else watch it … Yeah, well, I guess Lt. Bordeaux will just have to wait till I get back, won't he? Marla, look, I can't talk right now…"

He hung up and looked at Joe —who was still holding the liquor bottle in his hand— and said, "No, Joe, things are not okay… Andy and Chuck are still missing, for real. This is not a prank or any tricks to get 'extra' publicity for the TV station. I have everyone on my ass today. How much do I owe you?"

"Noting. These are on the house."

♦

Things should have not gone wrong like they did; Jim shouldn't have answered that phone call, at the beginning of the night shift.

Jim now tormented himself thinking he sent his crew to real danger; he probably sent them to something far worse.

He needed to think; he needed to go there … go to the same place he had sent his crew.

But he knew better than to go over there with the tape on him; he'd have to drop it in a safe place first.

Amariah opened the door, surprised to see him.

"Jim, hi. What's going on? What are you doing here? Gosh, you look like shit! Let me guess … You have been working the graveyard shift, again. When was the last time you slept?"

"Too damn long ago, Sis. Do you have some coffee for me? I need to talk to you about something…"

Jim was clearly in a very somber mood, when he walked inside his sister's house.

"Sure, I will make us a fresh pot. Come to the kitchen … Careful, don't step all over my cats like you usually do. Have you been drinking? I can smell it all over you. Does your wife know you've been drinking, again?"

"Damn cats of yours … What do you mean 'again'? I haven't had a drop for over twelve years now! And no, Marjorie doesn't know… What is this? A damn interrogation?"

They both went into Amariah's big kitchen.

She took the coffeepot out of a cabinet before turning to her brother and saying, "Well, that might very well be your story, but you sure smell like cheap bourbon. Pass that towel … Thanks. Er … no, I am not interrogating you; of course not… that's a wife's job. So what's going on? Shouldn't you be at home, or something at this time of the day?"

"Yeah … 'or something' is more like it," Jim said as he pulled out one of the chairs at the dining table and sat down.

"Well? Are you going tell me, or do I have to guess? Did you fight with Marjorie again? Did she kick you out of the house, yet again?" Amariah chuckled, amused.

"Last time she kicked me out of the house was in 1992 and I was drunk … No, it's not that."

"So, tell me Jimmy, what happened to the famous twelve steps? Did you stumble on step number eleven, dear?" Amariah openly laughed at her own joke.

"Damn it, Amariah, you know what? I always pitied Frank for putting up with you for so many years; you are too damn much to deal with ... I wonder if I should have gone straight home today, instead."

"Oh, yeah? Well, at least I'm not the one who ran away from home, upon turning fifteen, right? And for what? To sell newspapers in the corner of Myrtle and Studemont ... You always were a crazy S.O.B., you know that, Jimmy? Mom lost all hope for you, ever since."

"Well, I'm not here now to talk about that. I need a favor," Jim said, losing his patience.

If anyone knew how to make him feel vulnerable, by God that would be none other than his older sister Amariah. She was an absolute replica of their mother.

"Oh, well, I'm curious now," Amariah said, "We have barely talked to each other over the past five years, and now you need to ask me for a favor? This is new. So what is it, Jim?"

"I need you to conceal ... to hold on to something for me ... until I come to get it back. Can you do that for me?"

"Jim, is something wrong? Are you okay? You look spooked, boy." Amariah's tone softened.

"I take it you didn't watch the news last night." Jim said, in a dark mood.

"Last night was 'Poker Wednesday,' darling; I was busy playing cards with the girls, till late. Why? Was there something I should have watched?"

Amariah asked in a casual tone.

She walked closer to her brother, after waiting on his answer for a while.

"Jim, what is it?"

"Just hold on to this tape, and no matter what, don't watch it … you hear me? Don't. Talk to no one about it. I'm sure you will hear things. But don't talk about this tape to anyone, and hand it over to only me, when I come back to get it. Do you understand, Amariah?" Jim said, getting up from the chair.

She was surprised; she had never seen her brother behave like that.

"Yes … uh … yes, I do understand, Jim. Just answer this: are you and Marjorie okay? Are your kids okay?"

"They're fine … We are fine, thanks for asking. I knew I could trust you, Amariah. Listen, I gotta go now. You won't hear from me for a few hours … probably days, but it's okay. Thanks for doing this for me."

"Stay a little longer; coffee is almost ready, please. Don't leave like this; you don't look so good … If you don't want to talk about it, that's fine; just sit here with me for a while. It's lonely here without Frank around, you know? I don't get as many visitors like we used to." Amariah said putting the tape on the kitchen table.

"Okay. So, how's everything with you?" Jim was too worried to sit down and visit with his sister, but that was the least he could do, after asking her for such favor.

He looked around, the kitchen was spotless and somehow it reminded him of the kitchen of his childhood.

This one was yellow, flower curtains concealed the small window by the sink, the wallpaper had yellow and white motives; even the cookware and appliances were a pastel yellow.

Amariah gave him a fresh cup of coffee and poured one for herself, before answering, "Things are great, considering I have been a widow for the past five years, and I can still say I have two or three decent suitors waiting on me … Mom would be have been proud. Remember how much she hated Frank? And all I can say now is that he made me so happy, for all those years. Mother was wrong about him, you know, Jimmy?"

"You still miss Frank?" Jim said, trying to stay focused on the conversation; she deserved his attention, even if it was for just another minute.

There was a place he needed to go, before heading home.

"Would you miss Spring if we didn't have it one of these years? Of course I miss that bastard, Jimmy! He made me very happy. Up to the point where he got cancer, you know? After that I felt betrayed, but I stayed with him till the bitter end. What else could I do? You know all I went through. You and Marjorie were there for us ... He just was so sick...."

"Will you ever consider remarrying, Amariah? Marjorie says it's about time you moved on," Jim said, feeling true concern for his sister.

"Oh, I have moved on, all right; I have thirteen cats now ... They are a lot easier to deal with than men are, you know?"

She chuckled a little.


Jim Colby left his sister's house knowing he did the right thing; if Andrew and Chuck ever came back to tell their story, he would destroy that tape with his own bare hands -and would even bitterly laugh about the whole ordeal.

If only they would call Jim or the station back.

What was taking them so damn long?

After a two-hour drive Jim got on his cell phone to call his wife, Marjorie; he needed to let her know he was fine.

She was a worrier; she had always been.

Jim remembered that after Marla's call at the bar, he had turned his cell off, so he could get some peace of mind. He turned it on and after a few seconds, and it beeped indicating he had voicemail messages.

He checked to see: he had nine new messages.

# Amanda

"Please, Mrs. Jones, will you swallow that pill already?!"

"I don't see why they make pills so big, my Dear. They are not made for old women to swallow … What if it gets stuck in my throat? Would you know what to do then, young lady?"

"Oh, God! Of course I would, Mrs. Jones … I'm a nurse, in case you didn't notice."

Amanda tried hard not to lose her patience.

"Yes, I did notice, my dear, and a very pretty young girl, too. Did I show you my grandchildren's pictures yet? Hand me my bag, dear … They should be somewhere in there."

"Mrs. Jones … um … Dottie. I have been off shift for the past forty-five minutes … I have a family emergency I must attend to; I need you to swallow this pill before I leave. I know how hard it might be sometimes to take your medications, but your blood pressure will not come down any other way. It has been rather high for the past five hours, and if you don't follow the doctor's instructions I will have to—"

"Family emergency? What kind, dear?"

Dottie asked, truly concerned.

Amanda felt a lump in her throat, and fought back the tears. She had done that for so many hours now; she was tired and worried to death about Andrew, but could not give in to tears

At least not right now.

She thought to herself, *When would it be a good time for me to cry, oh God, when will it be a good time?*

"Is it your mom or dad, dear? Is it your son?" Mrs. Jones asked her, struggling with the pill in her mouth.

Her dentures gone, one could see the pill going from one side to the other, pushed in every direction by her tongue.

"I … no … er … I don't have any children. It's my boyfriend … my fiancé I am worried about."

Mandy thought she was losing the battle against tears, and forced a smile while wiping a furtive tear away.

She took a deep breath. She felt her face burning up.

Gosh, she was so tired and worried; if only she knew where Andy was.

Why hadn't he called her?

◆

Jim Colby was finally able to get to the right place; he looked at the house number, over and over again, while still in his car.

He took a worn-out piece of paper from his pants pocket and checked the address on it, against the house's address.

Yes, that was the right address.

It was a rather lonely road, now that he thought about it.

It must have been a scary route to drive at night.

As he approached the house he saw three police cars; which also gave enough indication Jim was at the right place.

It had to be.

He pulled over and saw the big numbers at the entrance.

The name of the street was right below the numbers. Andrew was right: he and Chuck had the correct address.

It was Jim who failed to double-check his source. And that was now proving to be a huge, costly mistake.

Jim got sighed and got out of his car.

He noticed yellow police tape all around the entrance of the property; Jim ducked as he passed under the tape in the front yard.

"Hey, you can't come in here … There's a police investigation going on."

A young police officer stopped Jim in his tracks.

"Yes, I know. I am James Colby, with the KLT TV station…"

"Oh, I see." The young police officer changed his tune and added, "Lt. Bordeaux is here somewhere ... He wants to talk to you. Please wait here, I'll go get him. Wait here," he insisted.

Jim had no intention of waiting for anyone, or talking to anyone. At least not just yet.

Whatever he knew, and whatever was on that damn tape didn't make sense at all; it all seemed to be taken out of a horror movie.

He had a few ideas of where he could start looking, but he was not going to share his information with the police.

He wasn't even sure about his source … It all had been odd from the beginning.

So odd.

◆

"Your fiancé? How lovely! Oh, well now, my dear, congratulations on your wedding!" Mrs. Jones said with a broad, toothless smile.

Mandy had to smile at the sight of the half-dissolved pill, still in Mrs. Jones mouth.

That helped her fight the tears that were brewing in her eyes, causing here to see double.

"You know what, Dottie?" Mandy said in a calm voice, "I think you are going to be all right. You don't have to swallow that pill anymore … Just keep it in your mouth, like you have been doing."

Dottie replied as she winced, "Are you kidding me, child? This pill tastes very bad. Gimme some water, please."

Half an hour later, Amanda drove to the TV station.

She lit up another cigarette with the one she had already smoked, to the very filter.

Upon lighting up the new one she thought to herself, *I should quit smoking. I promised Andrew I would ... I promised ... him.*

She pulled up the TV station's gate.

Amanda could not help but think of a few things as she approached that gate: that TV station was Andy's new workplace—he had been there for just six months.

The future looked so bright for him; she remembered that he had been assigned to the night shift, right away.

Mr. Colby —Andy's boss— said he was confident that Andrew would take over anchoring the evening news, in a couple of years ... Maybe sooner.

Jim always spoke highly of Andy.

Amanda and Andrew had met at the mall, she remembered; she had been drinking a soft drink at the mall's food court, when she first saw Andy.

He was sitting at another table, not far away from her.

He was reading some papers; he was so handsome, tall, blond ... She then wondered about the color of his eyes, and she smiled when he looked away from those papers, and she realized they were a clear blue.

Those eyes simply complemented his beautiful face; yes, it had been love at first sight.

She had told that story over and over, to friends and family. It still made her smile.

A little later in that same food court, Andrew looked at his watch and sprang to his feet. He was already late for something … She sighed upon seeing him leave; he never even saw her.

As he left, she noticed something on the chair next to the one he had been sitting in, a while ago. She smiled to herself in a devilish way; maybe not everything was lost.

She rushed over to pick it up.

It was a tie.

She ran after him, and as she approached him at the parking lot, she remembered the words they exchanged.

He said he was late for a job interview at a TV station … Would she like to talk about it over dinner?

Well, sure. Of course.


Amanda heard a distant thunder; it would rain soon.

A storm was also brewing in her heart. She sighed and looked up at the sky for answers: *Where are you, darling? Where can you be?*

She threw the last cigarette butt out of the window.

The incoming air blew her blonde curls wildly on her face; she tried unsuccessfully to control them with her free hand.

She held on to the steering wheel; her knuckles where white with anticipation. There were three cars in front of her, waiting their turn to pass the checkpoint at the TV station gate.

She needed answers and fast; she was losing her patience.

Amanda lit up a new cigarette and regretted throwing the last one out the window so impulsively. She waited some more.

She didn't roll the window back up; she needed fresh air—her face was on fire.

Mandy realized she was still wearing her nurse's uniform.

The only thing she could do at the moment was taking the name badge off. The sound of the squeaky wipers on the windshield made her aware that the passing rain had left, a while ago.

They were wiping on dry glass, and the screeching noise was intolerable.

She turned the wipers off, and waited a few more minutes, tapping her fingers on the dashboard; trying not to think, still fighting back tears.

She could not cry now; she was next in line. She wiped her face a little; the car ahead of hers was now in motion, going through the gate.

Amanda cleared her throat but did not throw her cigarette away this time. She held on to it, for self-assurance.

"Yes, ma'am?" the security guard at the gate asked, as he bent down to better look at her.

A distant thunder echoed. Mandy shook a little; the guard didn't seem to notice.

"I ... I ... am here to see Jim ... James Colby. My name is Amanda Sanders."

"Is he expecting you, Miss Sanders?" He asked while quickly glancing at the interior of the car, more out of habit than necessity.

"Yes … er … no … Listen, I talked to him a few hours ago. He knows I need to see him … Can you please let him know I'm here? Please?"

"Okay, wait here."

Amanda realized her cigarette had already consumed itself all the way to the filter; it was out now. She put it in the ashtray and realized her hand was shaking; the astray was full of cigarette butts and ashes.

She noticed the ring on her finger … the engagement ring Andy had given her, a couple of months ago. She couldn't do anything but feel her stomach tightening into a knot.

She stared at the security guard; he was still on the phone inside the inspection booth. She needed answers, and by God, she was not leaving the place without them.

What were her last words to Andy the evening before? Oh, yes, she now remembered: *"Take the umbrella; it's going to rain."*

Yes, those were her last words to him.

He mumbled something back on his way out, and then she heard the door slam behind him.

As she left for work sometime later, she realized the umbrella was still there. She had to smile; he was a fool, a total fool for getting a crazy job like this.

He must be a fool for wanting to marry her, after knowing each other for just a little over lousy six months.

He must have been a fool for going on any assignment Jim asked him to go to, no questions asked.

*Where was he now?*

♦

The house's front door was still wide open. Jim could see it, but it was too dark to be able to see the inside.

He would have to get closer.

As he walked further he noticed the news car still parked outside, it was the one Andrew and Chuck had driven, hours before.

The lights had been turned off … or maybe the battery was already worn out, after being on for so many hours.

The car doors had black spots where fingerprints had been lifted that very morning; police had opened the trunk, and the spare tire was out, on one side of the car.

Jim took a long look at the inside of the car: the keys were still in the ignition and two camera spare batteries were in the back seat.

He thought that was very ironic; those batteries were desperately needed, only hours ago.

The lives of his two men hung by a thread, due to a low battery. How odd to see these two fully charged, laying on the back seat.

"Hey!"

Someone yelled from behind Jim.

"Don't touch anything; we are still conducting an investigation here … Who are you anyway?"

A police officer in civilian clothes walked toward Jim. He wore plastic gloves and had a police badge on his pants belt.

"Sorry about that. I'm waiting on … er … Lt. Bordeaux. I'm here to talk to him," Jim lied.

"Oh, okay. Just don't touch anything … okay?"

The man warned. Jim nodded and the officer was soon gone.

Jim now turned his attention to the place, looking around; he recognized the surroundings.

Chuck had made sure to take those images for him the night before. Yes, it was clearly an abandoned place.

Jim then could do nothing but stare at the mansion. The color on its walls had faded away, a long time ago.

Jim could also see that wild plants had been crawling up the building for years: the grass was knee-high.

The place had clearly been abandoned for many years.

*How could he have sent his men there?*

He looked at the windows around the mansion, most of them were broken; the entrance had been very elegant, with a huge, wide wooden frame.

The door was thick and heavy, made of dark wood that seemed older than time; a broken marble bench stood nearby.

They remained the only silent witness to what might have happened the night before to his crew men.

Jim bent over and picked up a piece of marble from the ground, that little rock had once been part of the damaged bench; he put it in his pocket.

He did not want to forget that night, ever.

The piece of marble would be his constant reminder, until he solved the mystery.

Jim walked to the front door.

There were officers walking all around; no one seemed to be inside the mansion, at the time.

He pushed the door open with both hands, to take a better look inside; Jim realized the door was very heavy; he heard a squeaking noise coming from it.

He took a step further inside.

◆

"Ma'am!"

The word came to Mandy as a slap in the face. She snapped out of her own thoughts and looked at the guard, who was leaning over to her window.

She felt frightened for the first time, since all that craziness started.

"I'm s-sorry, what?" She whispered.

"Mr. Colby is not here." The guard informed her.

"Oh … but he must be ... He has to be."

She felt she was about to lose the little sanity that kept her troubled mind still glued together.

"I'm sorry, he's not; but don't worry his assistant said it's okay to let you in … her name is Marla Baines. Here, put this visitor badge on and go around that building; park your car in any of the assigned spaces labeled 'Visitor'… Are you okay?"

He seemed concerned.

Mandy was staring at her rearview mirror; she saw a police car behind her, waiting to get in next.

She saw two officers talking to each other and she wondered what they were doing there. Did it have anything to do with Andrew and Chuck?

"I'm f-fine, thanks. I will get going now," she said as she put the visitor badge on the passenger seat and started driving off.

She noticed as she pulled up slowly that the patrol car was let in without any further delay, and now they were driving right behind her.

She kept going, but could not ignore her heart pounding against her ribs.

She parked in one of the visitor spaces and waited a little while; the police car parked next to her. Two officers in uniform got out.

She lit up another cigarette; she realized she was shaking, but tried not to pay attention to her hands. She looked away after letting the white smoke go out, through her open window.

Amanda needed a minute to regain her confidence; she was not sure what awaited her, inside the building.

*Where could Jim Colby be?*

"… and so Jacob said they just vanished, man. They just did."

Amanda heard one police officer talking to his partner, through her open window.

She felt butterflies in her stomach. Probably it was more like nausea.

"What do you mean they just 'vanished', CJ? Nobody disappears like that, especially not with a camera and mike rolling ... You think it might be a trick?"

The other one said.

Amanda could not help listening in. She turned her head to hear better but she did not make eye contact; instead, she took her purse and pretended to look for something.

"I'm telling ya, John … unit 304 were the first ones at the scene after Colby called the dispatcher in, and there was nothing but an old, creepy abandoned building there …. And not the luxurious-looking house the reporter claimed to be at ... Jacob was there, he told me this first hand. I'm telling you man, all those boys were really spooked."

"For Christ's sake, CJ! Jacob is a wimp; he's always making up stories. I guess the TV crew went to the wrong place, simple as that."

"If that were the case, how do you explain their car parked at that creepy place with the lights still on, and both doors still open? It was very weird, I'm telling you. My wife saw the whole thing on the news last night … It could not be the same place they were broadcasting from. I don't know, John. These boys are still missing since last night … and this doesn't look good at all. Let's go in."

Both men walked off.

Amanda thought now might be a good time to cry; she couldn't help it anymore.

She knew she had heard enough, but she still didn't know what happened or how it all started. She just heard that they were still missing.

She just heard it firsthand from the police itself.

Nothing Marla Baines could say would make her feel better. Amanda felt a lump in her throat, and this time she wanted not to fight it back.

She needed to cry; she was desperate.

There was a light knock on her passenger window. Amanda jumped in her seat; her cigarette fell from her hand to the floor.

She looked at the passenger's window and saw Marla there, peeking through, and smiling a little. Mandy bent over to find the cigarette under her seat; she burnt her finger when she finally got it back.

She cussed and got out of her car as fast as she could. She forgot all about the tears, she forgot the lump in her throat, and that desperation she had felt moments before. And walked toward Marla, as she struggled to get rid of the cigarette.

She put her purse on her shoulder and attached the visitor badge to her nurse's uniform.

"Amanda, how good to see you," Marla said.

Marla Baines was in her forties, a small, petite brunette, impeccably dressed in a green business suit that made her eyes stand out, from her rather childish face.

Despite her looks, she seemed to have a very mature personality. She was a very much 'hands-on' woman.

Mandy realized all of a sudden how little she knew about this woman and her boss, James Colby. She knew very little, in fact, about her fiancé's job; she felt at a disadvantage.

She knew nothing of Andy's whereabouts up to that point, but she was sure that the woman shaking her hand might be her only way of finding out the truth.

Amanda—once more—fought back her tears.

Marla made small talk while they both walked inside the building.

As they went in, Mandy noticed that the cops were going inside an adjacent office, and closed the door behind them; the sign on that office read 'Executive Director.'

She tried to look for a name in her mind, a name that Andrew might have mentioned before.

*Who was the executive director at the company?* She felt like an idiot, for she did not know the answer to that.

Both women finally made it to a big office. Marla led the way, of course.

"Coffee or anything else?" Marla asked very politely and always with a big smile.

"No … I'm … I'm fine, thank you. Can I smoke in here?" Mandy said as she struggled to open her purse.

"I'm sorry, this is a non-smoking building." Marla said as they both sat down in Marla's office.

Amanda looked around; she realized it was her first time visiting Andy's new workplace.

"So, Amanda, how are you? I haven't had a chance to meet you before … Andy always talked a lot about you."

*'Talked'?*

How odd to hear Marla refer to Andy in past tense. Did Marla Baines know something Mandy didn't?

Most probably.

Maybe if Mandy paid close attention to whatever Marla said, she might understand what was going on.

She needed answers.

Although Mandy did not watch the news the night before, most of her co-workers had; and by God, they had only the strangest and most alarming things to say about the broadcast they all saw.

Andrew looked odd; he was lost, he could not find his way out … The equipment started to malfunction.

"Amanda?"

Marla's voice made Mandy come back to the present time; she looked at Marla and tried to smile while muttering an excuse for being so unfocused.

Amanda stood up and started to pace as she spoke.

"Marla … Marla, please tell me what's going on? I need the truth."

"We … ah … we are not sure at this time; it might be a little premature to say."

Marla tried to smile.

"Is Mr. Colby in? I must speak to him. Can I talk to him now?"

Mandy asked, trying to clear her mind.

"I'm sorry Amanda; he's not in right now … May I call you Mandy?"

Amanda nodded.

She sat down again; she felt that the news—or lack of it—was driving her insane. She felt as if her legs might not hold her any longer.

If that woman had indeed something to say, she needed to say it, right away.

Amanda looked elsewhere, she didn't feel strong enough to make eye contact.

"Mandy, we are trying to do everything we can; the police have been called in, and they are investigating now. Jim … Mr. Colby is also doing his own investigation; you have to trust him on this. I believe the police officers might want to talk to you too," Marla said as she pointed out to the executive director's door.

"What do you mean by that, Marla? I have no clue as to what happened last night! What could I possibly talk to the police about?"

Amanda was about to lose control. She took a deep breath before continuing.

"Look, I came in here to find answers not to give explanations about something I can't even understand! Is there anyone else I can talk to? Anyone else here, at all?"

Marla sat down next to Amanda and put her hand on Mandy's shoulder as she said, "Listen, I can assure you we are doing the best we can, everything we can … but the truth is … we haven't heard back from Andrew or Chuck since their last transmission, at the Fennigan mansion. We haven't heard anything at all."

Amanda ran her hand through her unruly blond curls.

Yes, this was just as good time to cry as any other, she thought.

Andrew was still missing and they had no idea how it happened. Marla had been no help at all; even if she tried talking to Marla, she had no information.

Amanda's thoughts turned to the conversation she overheard between the cops, back in the parking lot:

*... I don't know, John.... These boys are still missing since last night ... and this doesn't look good at all.*

Amanda started to cry inconsolably.

# The Phone Call

"Darling, you have not eaten any of the food I cooked for you," Marjorie told Jim, and continued, "Where were you all this time?"

"Is the morning paper in yet?" Jim asked.

"Oh, yes, it's got to be somewhere around here … I haven't read it; it has been a crazy morning here. The police called for you, and Marla, too. There, I see it…," Marjorie said pointing at the couch.

"I'll get it," Jim said as he walked away from the kitchen table.

He made no comment in regards to Marjorie's words. He was too busy in his own world, at the moment.

Strangely enough, he felt older; he had aged at least ten years in just a few hours.

He now felt the weight of all those years spent as a journalist, back when he ate, saw, and did nothing other than news broadcast.

All those years seemed to come back to rest very heavy on him - right between his shoulder blades- at that precise moment.

How could he forget the basics in journalism?

Always double-check you source, always!

How could he be so blind?

When did he let his guard down?

He remembered he felt a rather odd sensation minutes before talking to Andrew about the new assignment, the night before.

Jim should have paid closer attention to his second thoughts – and to his gut feeling.

He took the newspaper from the couch and unfolded it.

The headlines read:

## Local TV Crew Still Missing
## Case Re-opened at the Fennigan Mansion
## 9 People Now Missing Since 1973

James Colby had to sit down; he felt so tired and overwhelmed.

He read the article.

His hands were slightly shaking; Jim read as fast as he could.

Marjorie looked at him. She had not read the newspaper that morning, but as usual, she had seen the news the night before, and was fully aware of what was going on.

She did not ask any questions.

He seemed to have aged some since she last paid attention to his appearance. His dimples were deep as he pressed his lips in a fine line; he had not shaved in almost two days and the shade of a beard was already visible.

She wished he wouldn't worry so much about things; she still remembered the heart attack he had suffered, the year before.

All this grief and worry were not good for his health, and Marjorie worried.

"This is nothing but trash!"

Jim yelled as he threw the paper back on the couch.

He continued talking, more to himself than to his wife, "It's not fair. We still don't know what really happened out there, and they are speculating already about the fate of those two poor boys. It was not their fault at all; I should have checked out my source, before sending them there."

He turned to Marjorie and said in a low —and almost defeated— voice, "I should have checked it out first."

◆

As he took a long shower, Jim thought about the newspaper article.

There had been other people -over the years- going missing in that same house. And there was still an open investigation about those same disappearances.

An investigation that had been open for many years now -decades. It seems that place had been a 'cold case' for a very long time.

Jim remembered that only an hour ago, or so, he was about to step inside that very place, but a police officer stopped him, perhaps right on time.

What did they call that place in the newspaper?

Oh, yes, the 'Fennigan mansion,' that's right.

No one was allowed in the house, not even policemen; they all were very careful not to go inside. Maybe they knew something Jim didn't know; however, that didn't stop him from browsing as much as he could, while standing at the door.

That place didn't look anything like he had seen -the night before- on his TV monitor, back at the studio.

After shaving and getting dressed, James Colby went to the State Property and Real Estate Public Records Building; he was determined to find out as much as he could about the infamous Fennigan mansion.

As he left the house, Marjorie seemed distressed.

She asked him where he was going, but it was better that she didn't know; that way she wouldn't have any information to tell Marla -or the cops.

Marjorie reminded him that he had three messages from Marla and four from a police inspector.

Yes, of course, everyone wanted to talk to him. That was understandable; after all, he was the one who had taken the phone call that night.


As he drove in his car minutes later, he remembered how it all began.

It all came back to him very clearly.

He was getting ready to start producing the late evening news broadcast at 10:00 p.m., like he did every night.

He had been doing the night shift for the past twenty years, living life 'the other way around,' as Marjorie used to say, getting to work around 5:00 p.m. and coming back home next day around 4:00 or 5:00 a.m.

Marjorie used to say that while normal people worked the nine-to-five shift Jim had to do the nighttime one; Jim used to joke back, reminding her he was a 'night owl.'

She teasingly called him 'my sunrise guy,' since that was the time at which he showed up at home, every day.

The night before, Jim was at the audio cabin making sure the broadcast would go smoothly, testing some equipment there.

They still had a few hours before going on air, but Jim was a perfectionist.

The phone there rang; one of his audio engineers motioned to answer it, but since Jim was next to the phone he said, "It's okay, I got it."

Life for him and others would never be the same again, after that one call.

As Jim Colby picked the phone up, he heard an ongoing conversation between a man and a woman. The lines were obviously crossed, or so it seemed.

Instead of hanging up —and minding his own business— the journalist in him couldn't help but listen.

"I'm telling you, we keep on hearing these very strange noises in my basement; that's where the wine cellar is … you know?" The woman said.

She seemed very distressed.

"Yes, ma'am, I understand."

Jim heard the man replying. That man had a very strange foreign accent; oriental perhaps.

"I'm throwing a big party tonight at home … Both the Governor and Major will be here tonight, and I can't have these horrible, weird noises ruining everything! I just will not have that! It sounds like there is something terrible happening downstairs and the maids are terrified to go in the cellar. They simply refuse… We need to take care of this and fast. Is there any way you can send someone over, right now?"

"Yes, ma'am, I can." The man responded in a rather unconcerned voice.

Almost an impersonal voice.

"Look, these noises are rather… very odd… if you know what I mean. There could be something very big, down there. Send someone fully prepared for whatever they might encounter in the cellar. Whatever it is has been there for a few weeks now… Your men will have to deal with it right there… Get rid of it; terminate it… Do you understand? I want it gone, dead and vanished. Hurry, please… My name is Mary Fennigan and my address is …"

James Colby found himself writing down her name and address; it seemed like a very odd phone call.

Jim was most intrigued to find out what was 'down there,' making all those weird noises.

The phone call between the woman and the man ended as soon as she gave him her address and the man promised to send someone at once. He'd send someone 'fully prepared' … But for what?

Who was the man? What kind of job did he have that had him going into a wine cellar and taking care of whatever commotion was down there that had the servants 'terrified'?

Jim Colby took the piece of paper with the address and walked out of the sound cabin, he was distracted, reading his notes and trying to think about what he had just heard, still trying to figure out what just had happened.

He found himself going to Andrew Wallace's desk.

Andy was his 'new' special investigations reporter. Andrew was a man in his early twenties, very hyperactive, a smile on his face all the time, and always willing to investigate anything and go anywhere Jim sent him, without asking any questions—always so trusting.

Jim didn't know much about this guy. His resume was good. Not real impressive, since Andrew was just getting started in life and new career; however, he seemed to be intelligent and outgoing, though very reserved when it came to his private life.

Upon checking Andy's references, Jim realized people had only compliments to give about Andy.

Jim knew Andrew had a girlfriend; there were marriage plans in the near future, but nothing concrete as of yet. At least, not that Andy had mentioned any plans to Jim.

As for Andy's family, Jim had no idea about his parents or siblings. Andy did not talk too much about himself; he'd answer questions but not volunteer any personal information, on his own.

Jim remembered the job interview he had with Andrew Wallace, only a little over five months ago—or was it six already?

Andrew was Jim's fourth interview of the day; it had been raining all morning and Jim's mood was not the greatest. The other three candidates had all a background in broadcasting, anchoring, investigations, etc.

This next guy had no background in TV, radio, or even printed journalism, but he seemed to be a good writer.

Andrew wrote a few articles for the *Gazette,* back when he was in college.

Of course, you can't consider the '*Gazette*' a newspaper. If anything, it was a lousy college social magazine, but he would give this boy a chance—at least an interview.

After all, if the boy seemed right, Jim could mold him -make him from scratch, just like Jim himself had started, so many years ago.

Jim especially wouldn't have to put up with any attitude or 'great ideas' the other candidates might like to throw, to impress him. He wanted someone fresh and trainable for that position.

In the end, Andrew seemed the best choice.

Jim now tried to remember the interview at Joe's bar.

"You are from … er … New York. Right?" Jim started the interview and asked, "What brings you to this tiny town in the middle of Pennsylvania, boy?"

"A friend of mine lives here … He's the one who told me about this position being open … uh … This friend of mine actually works for you," Andy said with a smile.

"Is that right? Who is your friend?"

"Chuck … Chuck Robbins. He's the cameraman, in the night shift."

"Oh, yes, Chuck, I know who he is … And how did you guys meet?"

"We went to school together; he's from New York, too."

"I see. Do you miss the 'Big Apple'?"

"Nah, not really. I'd like to find work here."

"Fair enough. Do you have any experience in front of a camera? I'm looking for a reporter, you know? For special investigations … Someone I can send out in the field; someone who will not be afraid to make an interview. To be honest with you, what I am looking for is someone who can get to a crime scene even before the cops get there, and be able to pull the interview before anyone else from our competitors. I'm looking for initiative, someone daring."

"I understand," Andy said.

"You think you can do it?" Jim asked, after a while.

"Yeah, I can. I'm your man. If you give me a chance, I know I can do it," Andy's face lit up; he seemed sincere.

"Okay, boy.… I'm going to give you a chance. Here's my card. Tell Marla, my assistant, you got the job; ask her to show you where you desk is. Don't expect nothing fancy; just do a good job and we'll go from there. Now go. I have a few things to do today and Marjorie wants me home early; we are having company … uh … Marjorie is my wife."

Jim cleared that for Andy.

"Thank you, sir … Mr. Colby. Thank you very much. I promise I won't let you down; I'll do my best."

Jim left a couple of bills on the table, to pay for the coffee he had drunk all afternoon. He started walking for the door.

As he folded Andy's resume and placed it in his jacket pocket, he replied without turning his head to Andrew, "Welcome to KLT.… Oh! And Andrew…?"

Jim stopped with the door halfway opened, and turned around as he smiled devilishly.

"Yes, sir?" Andy asked as he got up from his chair.

"I forgot to tell you … I got you set up for the night shift."

# The Investigation

"Yes, sir, may I help you?"

"Yes, I need to talk to Fred Cornelius. My name is Jim Colby."

"Please be seated; he's in a meeting right now, but I will let him know you are here … Do you have an appointment?"

"No … I don't have one. I'll wait. Thanks," Jim said as he walked to the waiting room.

"Can I get you some coffee … or water?" The receptionist asked.

"No, no, I'm fine, thank you." Jim turned around to respond.


Jim then sat down on one of the chairs; he took a magazine from the coffee table, and stared blankly at it.

A minute later he put it back down. He could not read or think of anything else other than what was going through his mind at that moment.

He needed some answers, and that phone call had to be the answer he needed.

That damn phone call.

He recapitulated his tracks a bit, to make sure he was on the right path: Fred was Director of the State Property and Real Estate Public Records Building; he would be able to help him find information about the Fennigan mansion.

Fred would surely give Jim access to those files. That was a good start.

What else can Jim do?

Well, he would have to check with the phone company next, of course; he needed information about where the call was placed from.

Was it really a crossed line, or was that call made on purpose to the TV station? What if one of his competitors was behind this hideous prank?

God! He was paranoid now … and the last thing he needed was to be paranoid.

What was the name of the girl? Gosh, he tried to think of something else; he had to.

Andrew's girl, yes; he talked on the phone to her, only hours ago.

What was her name again? Mandy … Amanda! That's it, Amanda. He could not remember her last name, but he was grateful to have something else to think about.

Jim wondered if he'd eventually have to talk to Andrew's parents, later on.

What would he tell them?


His cell phone rang inside his jacket pocket. He jumped to his feet; he started to pace around the room.

He had kept the cell phone on, after hearing all his messages at home.

Jim was not ready to give answers. At least not before doing his own investigation, but yes, he was ready to face the world … or at least try to buy some more time.

After all, he was the only one to blame for what happened.

There were no records anywhere in the TV station showing where he got his info from, no records at all.

And that was why the police were looking for him. Jim had a few leads and he'd use all available resources to his advantage.

"Hello?" Jim answered his cell phone.

"Mr. Colby … this is Marla. Are you okay?"

He heard his assistant's voice on the other end.

"Yes. What is it, Marla?"

Jim seemed eager.

"Er … there's a young lady here to see you."

Marla sounded a little nervous, but Jim didn't seem to notice.

"Have her make an appointment for some other day. How's everything over there? Do I have any calls?" Jim asked.

"Well, yes, some calls; but those can wait. You see, this young lady is Andrew's fiancée … Amanda, and she needs to talk to you … She's not doing very well right now."

Marla tried to give Jim a hint on how things were on her end.

"Gosh … I was just thinking about her. Any word on Chuck's family yet?"

"Yes, Jim. I was able to track  his aunt down. Chuck has no parents. He was raised by his aunt Margaret; she's an old lady, and she told me on the phone she could not make the trip over here … She's waiting to hear back from us, when we find something out."

"I see … Tell Amanda I'm trying to find out more. I can't go to the office now to see her. Are the police still all around the place?"

"Er … yes, they are."

She sounded rather stiff.

"Mainly looking for me?"

Jim needed to know.

"They have a warrant," Marla said, lowering her voice now.

"For me…?"

Jim stopped pacing around the waiting room. Placing him under arrest now would be a very bad thing.

He needed time.

"For the tape," Marla said.

"Don't worry then … Tell Amanda … Mandy to go home. We will call her as soon as we know more. There is no point in waiting over there."

"I don't … I don't think she wants to leave right now. I mean … she is determined to talk to someone here."

Marla insisted, feeling sorry for the girl sitting in front of her.

"Marla … please, I don't have time for that now," Jim said, losing his patience.

"I understand," Marla said with a sigh.

"Keep me posted on things there … I don't want to talk to the police. At least not yet."

Jim hung up.

Jim looked at Fred's secretary; the view was a little odd. She was a rather large woman, sitting behind a very small desk.

She smiled at him and told him Fred Cornelius would see him, in a few minutes; Mr. Cornelius was wrapping up his current meeting.

Jim thanked her and picked up the same magazine he had put away minutes before.; he thought he could use a drink, too.

Jim twice caught the secretary looking at him with a mixture of suspicion and curiosity.

Damn town; very tightknit community.

Gossip and rumors flew in that place so fast it was unbelievable. Most likely she knew who Jim was, and maybe she was aware of what was going on.

She probably watched last night's events unfolding on her TV, too.

Sometimes it was tough to live in such a small place.


*Why in the world did he ever come to live here?*

Yes, it had been because of her: Marjorie.

She was his reason for doing so many things in life; she was his reason for living, his reason for joining AA and giving up alcohol, years before. She was also his reason to survive that damn heart attack, the previous Summer.

She was the sun of his life, and yes, she had refused to move out of that tiny town in Pennsylvania, back when they first met, many years ago in Chicago.

It only seemed natural to stay there with her.

His cell phone rang again. He thought of turning it off after that one call, or the phone would never stop ringing.

He looked at the caller ID. It was his sister Amariah.

"Jim? Where are you, dear?"

She sounded stressed.

"I can't tell you that. What is it?"

"I'm worried about you."

"No need for that. I'm fine."

"Jimmy, there was a cop coming here, earlier. He asked me about you … He's long gone now but I kept thinking why look for you here, you know?"

"What did you tell him?" Jim asked and turned his back to the receptionist, in case she might be listening to his conversation.

"Jim … are you in trouble with the police? Are you having some kind of problem?"

She needed to know.

"What did you tell him?"

Jim insisted.

"Well, nothing of course! He wanted to know where to find you. I told him I didn't know … and that's pretty much the truth; I have no clue where you can be, other than home or work."

"And that's all they need to know for now, Amariah."

"Are you running from the law, James Colby? Now, tell me the truth!"

Amariah started losing her patience; she felt somehow responsible for her younger brother.

"Oh, hell, no. I'm not in trouble, Amariah. Just remain calm, okay?"

He tried to sound convincing.

"Does that have anything to do with the tape you gave me this morning?"

" Listen …" Jim started looking for the right way to make her understand what he needed from her.

"No, you listen to me, Jim … I want you to know that no matter what, I'll keep the tape in a safe place, and I will not even hand it over to your own wife! I trust your judgment; I know you can be crazy sometimes, but I'll keep my word."

There was sheer determination in her tone.

"Thanks, Amariah. I'll talk to you later."

"Jim? Please, take care of yourself."

They hung up.

James was not sure if he had done the right thing by giving the tape to his sister; after all, they were not that close, not anymore.

But if he ever doubted his sister, he knew better now.

She would not give the damn tape away, not to anyone but him; that tape contained perhaps the last minutes in the lives of two men, his crew.

That tape might hold the answer to something Jim did not understand; something perhaps unnatural or perhaps a crime in progress.

It was hard to say which.

Jim wanted to review that tape the night before at the studio, right after he sent the second crew to the scene, where the first one had turned up missing.

He wanted to go to his office, lock the door, and view the whole thing over and over, frame by frame, until he could come up with some answers.

A logical explanation.

But he knew that as soon as the horrific transmission was over police would be knocking at his door, but Jim could not release the tape for the world to see.

Right now only a few hundred had seen it; they saw what happened live, when he made a mistake—a big mistake—and told Andrew they'd broadcast the investigation live.

Jim love the shocking factor in a story, the surprise in action. So he decided to go live with this one.

And live they went, only to broadcast the horrific fate of his men and for that, he was responsible, and would pay whatever price he had to.

But he'd protect people like Amanda and Chuck's aunt from seeing it, at least unless he found out what exactly had happened to his crew.

Jim reviewed in his mind the investigation the second crew did at the 'crime scene,' the night before.

They arrived at the exact location where the first crew was last heard of, and seen from; they videoed Andy and Chuck's car, just as they left it, minutes before.

His second TV crew found the front door wide open, and they, too, went inside the house.

That place was so odd, so different from the one the boys had broadcasted, earlier. The police arrived within a few minutes and ordered his second crew immediately out of the house.

"Jim!"

The sound of Fred's voice made him jump to his feet.

Jim was so lost in those feelings and thoughts that he didn't hear his friend coming in.

But Fred was not alone, not at all; and before Jim could say anything Fred said, "It's good to see you Jimmy… This is Lt. Bordeaux, and this is Officer Smith. They are here for the same reason you are. Gentlemen, please come with me."

# The Fennigan Mansion

Fred Cornelius had been working at the State Property & Real State Building for over forty years. He had been friends with Jim and Marjorie Colby for a long time, too.

Fred knew where he stood when it came to Jim asking for a favor, especially one as big as this one.

Fred was a rather large man, in his early sixties; he was always trying to quit smoking his cigars but always kept one in his pocket, just in case.

Sometimes Jim would tease Fred about it. It was clear that when Fred was stressed out he would hold the cigar in his hand and maybe place it in his mouth by force of habit; however, he never lit it up.

"Jim, these gentlemen have a warrant to see information on the Fennigan property … I'm not going to lecture you now, but you need to know that all information on the property is confidential. The only way to access it is with a warrant -like the one these gentlemen have now. I talked to them and they have no problem with you being here … in their investigation. They know who you are, Jim."

Jim froze; he knew the jig was up, but somehow he managed to say, "I thank you for this favor, Fred. I need to know what happened to my crew..."

Jim then turned to the officers and said, "Gentlemen, I will be more than happy to answer any questions you might have, or even go with you to—"

Officer Bordeaux interrupted Jim, "We are not here to talk to you, Mr. Colby, or take you down to the station. There's no warrant issued for you, that we know of. We believe you are here for the same reasons we are, and I think you have as much right as anyone else to know what happened to your men. However, I'd like to have a word with you, after we are done here. Mr. Cornelius, if you would be kind enough to show us the way."

"Of course, Lieutenant. Please, this way…."

Fred walked in front of the group, and his right hand went instinctively to the pocket where the fine cigar was. He then cleared his throat.

All kinds of thoughts went through Jim's mind as he walked down the corridor with his friend, and the other men.

He was not worried about himself; he was a little scared about what they might find out … or perhaps what they might not find, that would not answer all the questions everyone had.

If that were the case, then the police would be back to square one, and square one was he: Jim Colby.

He knew police would be very thrilled to ask him why he sent the men to the Fennigan mansion, in the first place.

How did he come up with the idea?

So many questions for which he had no answers.

"Did any of you watch the transmission … last night?" Jim asked as soon as they all went inside a small elevator.

Fred pushed the button to go down, toward the file-storage room at the basement.

There was a short, uncomfortable silence.

Officer Smith finally spoke up, "I did. Yesterday was my night off… I was home. My wife was very distraught after the transmission was unexpectedly cut off. We thought the whole thing might have been a publicity stunt, or something … This morning my partner and I were assigned to the Fennigan mansion case, and lemme tell you that place doesn't look like anything your men showed on TV, last night, Mr. Colby. I still believe they went to the wrong house, or somethin'. They are somewhere else… they have to be."

Jim then turned around and found the men avoiding any eye contact with each other; it was an odd, and very uncomfortable situation for all.

They waited for the elevator to reach their floor, at the bottom of the building; Smith started to bite one of his fingernails nervously.

The elevator doors finally opened and the men walked toward a well-illuminated floor with a few desks here and there; all of them were empty.

Except for three clerks there, the whole floor was empty.

Large file cabinets lined up against the walls; the place seemed old but was kept neat and clean.

A musky odor filled everyone's nostrils. Jim noticed the odor resembled that of old oak.

"I had this place evacuated."

Fred started saying, as if answering a question that was never formulated.

He showed the men the way.

"That's very good, Mr. Cornelius; the fewer people that know the details of our investigation, the better off we are for now," Lt. Bordeaux said as he took a little black book from his pants pocket to start taking notes.

He seemed interested in the place.

"That's what I thought," Fred replied.

They approached one of his clerks and he said, "Susan ... please give us the room for a few minutes; we'll be using your computer for a while. Take a break."

The clerk took her purse and left, not without looking at every man with curiosity; it was as if she was trying to gather all information she could -to tell her friends later in the coffee shop, after hours.

Fred sat down on the small chair. He was a heavy man; the chair squeaked as he sat down.

He placed his chubby fingers on the keyboard and punched in some codes, to get to the screen he needed.

Everyone seemed rather stressed out. Jim's throat was dry.

After a few minutes -that lasted an eternity- Fred clapped his hands together, while staring at the screen and said, "Ok, I'm in ... Let me double-check the address. Jim?"

Jim Colby took a piece of paper from his shirt pocket; it seemed a very old piece of paper, but in truth it was worn out from so much handling.

Jim cleared his throat and realized now just how dry it really was. He read the address aloud.

Fred turned to the officers for confirmation.

"Is this the same address you have, Lt. Bordeaux?"

Lt. Bordeaux had his own piece of paper to double-check the address ... It was the warrant for the tape. He nodded after reading it.

"Okay then," Fred said as he keyed the address in.

After a few seconds he said, "There's only one location and property that corresponds to that physical address; there is no mistake. If both parties went to the same address then it must be this one here. The house known as the Fennigan mansion...."

There was silence as if everyone there needed to absorb that information.

Fred sighed and he then continued:

"It was last rented to a family ... hmm ... the Ulhman's ... in 1979 ... But according to this, they did not even last three months there. Let's see ... prior to that, the house belonged to a Sam and Mary Fennigan. They lived there in ... in ... the early thirties ... from 1929 to 1935, according to this data. They left for Europe sometime in the fall of 1935, and the house was put on the market three years later... It seems The Fennigans did not comeback ... hmm ... well, gentlemen?" Fred asked, looking up at everybody, searching for clues as to what to do next.

Fred was feeling more apprehensive by the minute.

Although he did not dare to say it in the elevator, truth was that Fred and his wife watched the news broadcast the night before and they, too, watched the whole thing, in earnest surprise. Not knowing what to make out of that 'investigation.'

Fred was aware of what was going on; it didn't take a rocket scientist to realize the problem these men currently had in their hands.

Jim cleared his throat -once more- before speaking, "Is that all, Fred?"

He asked in a low voice. Visibly disappointed.

Fred started clicking away with the mouse as if trying to find out more. Changing screens at the speed of light.

He answered Jim's question while looking at the monitor, "Yup, so it seems ... This is a very old property. According to this, Sam Fennigan bought the land in 1926 and it took about two years to build the house ... er ... mansion. I see here some reports from the construction inspectors of that time, one report was made in 1926 and another one in 1927 ... I take it the mansion was still under construction during those two years."

"How big was the property and construction....?" Lt. Bordeaux asked Fred.

Fred scrolled up and down. He was sweating now; he wanted to help with the investigation but he also felt he needed to get some fresh air, or maybe just go back to his office.

Anywhere but there.

Nothing there made sense.

"Let's see ... hmm ... ah, here it is: total property was 32,550 square feet ... with 15,600 square feet of construction. Three story-house. Damn, it's a very large house ... like one of those country-club houses or something..."

Jim leaned over the desk and asked, "Is there a way to look at the floor plan? Do you keep a copy, somewhere in here?"

Jim was starting to feel nervous; he had thought earlier that the answer he was looking for would be a simpler one, an easier one.

He had been wrong.

But still, there had to be something to go by, somewhere.

"That's a good idea, Colby," Lt. Bordeaux said.

Fred looked at Jim, trying to think; he then looked at the officers before responding, "Well, sure, I guess ... but I don't see how the floor plans have anything to do with—"

Jim interrupted Fred by saying, "It's important, Fred. We have footage of the inside of the house … and that damn house changed a lot within two hours; that I can tell you."

Jim took his handkerchief out of his jacket pocket and wiped his forehead.

Was it hot in there or was it just him? He felt he couldn't breathe.

Officer Smith approached Jim and asked, "So, there IS a tape. We knew it all along but haven't been able to track it down, at your TV station. Do you have it, Mr. Colby?"

Jim looked at him, and then at the other officer; they knew.

Their eyes locked, and after a few seconds, Jim decided to follow Fred to one of the filing cabinets nearby.

Jim was aware that the officers were still waiting for his answer.

"It's in a safe place … for now," Jim finally said, without looking at either man.

"You could get into big trouble for withholding evidence from us, Colby… I'm sure you know we have a warrant issued here to get that tape," Bordeaux said, looking at Jim over Smith's shoulder.

"I thought you said you were not here to get me," Jim confronted Bordeaux.

Smith was caught up in the middle, and grew nervous by the confrontation of the two men.

Officer Smith decided to step aside, and get out of the way.

"You want to be very careful with all this, Colby. I must remind you of your position here … It doesn't look too good; your men are still missing and you are the one who sent them to that creepy place, where they encountered God knows what."

"Are you suggesting I sent them to that damn place, knowing they'd be in danger?"

Jim was so close to Bordeaux that he could clearly see the small scar on the officer's left eyebrow.

Bordeaux did not step back; he too meant business.

"Look, Colby, all I'm saying is ..."

Fred interrupted the argument, "Gentlemen, please, please; this is hardly the place and time to discuss any of that. Look," Fred said as he showed the men," I found the book where the floor plans should be... Well?"

Fred asked when he realized Bordeaux and Jim were still looking at each other, in open confrontation.

Fred continued speaking, "Do you want to see the book, or shall I call it quits, and go back to my office?"

Fred was starting to feel annoyed with the situation.

He took his handkerchief out of his chest pocket, making sure he did not drop his precious cigar. His forehead was full of tiny drops.

After a few more seconds, both men moved toward the large table where Smith—biting a fingernail off—was already looking at the faded-blue old prints Fred was already unwrapping for them.

Bordeaux pushed Smith a little to the side; Smith bumped into Jim, who was also trying to find a good place to look at the blueprints.

Smith stayed put between the two men and looked down again, finding another fingernail to bite off.

"Damn, this looks like an Egyptian papyrus or something…," Fred said, trying to get the men off the previous argument.

He then pointed out as he stated, "The whole thing is crumbling … but here, look … this house was big, and I mean big: eleven bedrooms upstairs, on the third floor. Another nine rooms on the second floor, an interior patio downstairs with what seemed to be a fountain or statue in the middle … some benches around it … Let's see.… How many rooms on that first floor?" Fred talked to himself as he moved his chubby, right index slightly above the blueprints, trying to avoid touching the old floor plan.

"Here … seven bedrooms on the first floor. There were three levels total… Ah! That is incorrect. This here seems to be an underground level, which would add an extra floor to the house, with a total of four floors."

Fred looked up at the three men and explained further, "Although people don't count basements and attics as house levels, in this case the basement ran as large and wide as any of the other 3 floors, therefore it will be considered as a floor, not a space." Fred said in a deep voice, as if he were deciphering old hieroglyphs for tourists at the museum.

"That's the cellar. It's where the wine cave was and where the Asian man was sending his men," Jim said without thinking.

He pressed his lips together as if to stop himself from saying anymore, thus incriminating himself further.

All three men looked at him in surprise. Jim realized his mistake. He avoided eye contact with any of them.

"Have you been there before?" Smith asked with morbid curiosity.

There was a smirk on his face.

"No."

Was all Jim could say.

He was rather upset at his own stupidity.

"I thought you said you didn't know where you were sending your men," Bordeaux said as he squinted at Jim.

Bordeaux slightly pushed Smith out of his way, and slowly walked to Jim.

Jim rolled his eyes while thinking, *Oh, God! Here we go again.*

He didn't want confrontation—not that he was going to run from a fight, if provoked.

Once more, Fred saved his butt from being chewed out by Bordeaux.

"Well … you are right, Jim. According to this." Fred kept going as he moved his finger to another page, he then continued speaking, "Yes, this whole area was the cellar and here … was the wine cave."

Fred looked at Jim, rather surprised.

Fred put his wet handkerchief back into his jacket pocket and took the cigar out, without even thinking about it.

He held it in his chubby fingers. After that, Fred could do nothing but look up to Jim as if waiting for an answer.

Jim walked off to the elevator.

Bordeaux was the first to react, and walked after Jim.

"Wait! Not so fast, Colby!"

Jim pushed the button to go up, without even looking at Bordeaux; he was not running away.

"I am afraid you can't leave this place, Colby," Bordeaux said.

Jim looked at him; his mind was made up.

He said, "I will not be held against my will by you or anyone … especially without a warrant for my arrest."

The elevator doors opened; Bordeaux blocked the way as he told Jim, "Colby, don't do this; you know we can hold you and take you down to the station, if we have to; and besides ..."

Jim sighed and cut him off in mid-sentence, "I don't care what you think you can or cannot do, Bordeaux. You know that if you take me in right now, after one phone call to my lawyer I'd be back on the street, in no time. So no, I am not going with you. Instead, you are coming with me."

Fred took his lighter out of his pocket; this whole thing was just too much.

That was as good time as any other to light up his damn cigar.

# The Crew

Andrew was very excited about his new job; he was sure things would change for him very soon … and for Mandy, too.

They were in love and the future looked promising for both. Mr. Colby had assigned him to the night shift; his team buddy was none other than Chuck, his longtime good friend.

All Chuck and Andy had been doing so far were short investigations on government corruption, a police sting, a few cases of police brutality, and a drug bust … nothing 'big' yet.

But he was sure one of these days Jim Colby would send him to something important; and yes, it would be their chance to break through, in live media coverage.

Chuck, on the other hand, was a rather lonely man; he had few friends and didn't care for a girlfriend, after the last one left him heartbroken.

In Andy's opinion, Chuck was the best of friends; he was an expert when it came to using the camera—a 'camera geek,' as Andy used to call him.

Chuck loved to go outside the TV studio and take shots at anything: a nice sunset, the stars, a car wreck, a bar fight … anything he found interesting.

Chuck had a real passion about getting everything on tape and he had been showing Andrew lately how to use the camera, in case he ever had to use it.

"And besides," Chuck used to say, "it was always useful to be familiar with the gear and tools you work with. The tools of the trade."

That afternoon was not special at all; it was a Wednesday like any other. The only interesting thing at the TV studio was the weather broadcast: rain soon would be rolling in.

Andy was rather bored that day; he had been working on a couple of leads for a story, nothing fancy. After six months on the job, he realized what a small town that was; there were not too many things happening there, at least not at once.

It was not like in New York, where you had to cut material and news off, for lack of airtime. Too many good stories but you had to choose only the best ones, and squeeze them in a one-hour news broadcast.

No, this was a very different place; you basically struggled every day to get good material for the special nightly edition, and to go on air live was an even harder thing to do.

The story had to be very good for that.

That Wednesday night, Andrew was playing with a pen between his fingers, sitting at his desk, working on the only two stories he currently had. Those stories were too ordinary and a bit boring. He was aware he needed something else.

Something with a kick, something that might 'wow' the audience.

The past two nights all he had to do was deskwork. Colby would not let him air because he didn't have enough material to go on.

Andy hated that.

What if Colby decided to lay him off?

Andy would not tell Amanda about his worries; she worked the night shift, too, but at the local hospital, and she didn't keep track of the times Andy went on air, live.

He figured she must have sensed something was not right with him; but if she did, she wouldn't ask any questions -and for that, Andy was grateful.

"Hey, Andy!" Jim Colby said walking toward Andy's desk.

Andy straightened up in his chair, looked up and smiled some.

"Yes? What is it, Mr. Colby?"

"Jim, call me 'Jim.' Damn it, I can't believe after all these months working for me you still can't call me 'Jim.' "

Andrew got nervous, thinking Colby was there to ask about the material he might have for that night.

Oh boy, he was going to be very disappointed upon hearing he had nothing to go on that night, either.

"Uh … yes, Jim … sorry … er … I was just…." Andy started to try to explain, but he didn't have to.

Jim interrupted him, "Yes, that's better, boy. Listen, I have something here for Chuck and you … How busy are you boys, tonight? This here looks promising. You might go live on this one, depending on how things look when you get there," Jim said while holding a piece of paper in his fingers.

Andy stood up and said, "Oh, well, we were working on some stories … but that can wait." Andy had a broad smile when he asked Jim, "What is it?"

"Call Chuck and get your butts in my office, in five minutes. I'll meet you both there," Jim said as walking away.

"Yes, sir! I mean … Jim!"

Jim smiled as he walked to the coffee dispenser to get more caffeine; if things went the way he thought they would, he was in for a long and exciting night.

Jim was right; it turned out to be a very long night. Sprinkled with a lot of excitement, too.

Only it was the wrong -worst- kind of excitement any one could ever expect.

All in all, Jim got a lot more than he bargained for.

♦

"Well? Where are we?" Jim heard Bordeaux asking, in a rather impatient voice.

Lt. Bordeaux still could not believe he let Jim Colby talk him into such craziness.

Jim's 'plan' was against police procedure, and what got Bordeaux the most was that the whole thing also went against his policeman's instincts.

*Since when do we let suspects run the show?* - He asked himself.

"The phone company," Jim said, turning off his car's engine.

He saw Smith's face in his rearview mirror. Smith spat out a chunk of fingernail.

"I still don't understand what we are doing here," Smith protested from the back seat.

He too seemed uncomfortable.

"You'll see."

Jim said getting out of the car and walking off, without waiting for them.

The two police officers looked at each other for a second or two, maybe in disbelief, maybe trying to check on each other.

Truth was they still didn't have a chance to discuss -among themselves- what was going on. Their investigation had taken an unexpected detour, they didn't know if this would go someplace or nowhere at all.

They followed Jim without any further delay.

They all got in the building and Jim talked to the receptionist briefly.

Smith took that opportunity to approach Bordeaux and asked, "So, Chief, what do you think?"

"I am not sure right now what to think. It's clear that Colby knows more than what he has told us, but I'm not sure what it is. I have no idea how this investigation has a link with this place, but I'm sure we will find out. Keep an eye on him; he might try to ditch us."

Smith nodded and both men started to walk toward Jim.

All three remained in silence at the waiting room; they did not talk to each other at all.

Jim was lost in his thoughts for what seemed an eternity; after a while he checked his cell phone for messages.

Bordeaux paced in front of Jim, as if to remind Jim, he was not going anywhere until Bordeaux got the answers he needed for his investigation.

A few minutes later a young man, dressed up in a brown suit, came out of the elevator to greet the men.

"Mr. Colby, how good to see you!"

The employee said in a cheerful voice.

"It's good to see you too, Larry. How's your dad? Still climbing on phone poles?"

Jim said, walking past Bordeaux.

Jim didn't even bother to introduce the police officers to Larry; Bordeaux and Smith followed Jim closely, behind the clerk.

"Oh no, Mr. Colby, not anymore. Dad retired after he fell from one of those in 1996 … Ah … this way, please," Larry said when he realized the other two men were also coming along.

Jim followed Larry through some corridors.

Larry finally opened a large door and asked as he let the men in, "Can I get you gentleman something to drink … some coffee, perhaps?"

All three men stopped and Jim said, "I don't think I need anything right now; thanks, Larry."

Jim turned his head and looked at his companions. Both declined coffee as well.

"Mrs. Hall will be with you shortly; let me know if you need anything else, gentlemen. It's good to see you again, Mr. Colby. Please say hi to your wife from me."

The clerk smiled as he closed the door behind him.

As Larry left the room, Smith began to pace and bite his fingernails - yet again.

Jim sat down on a single chair, openly avoiding sitting at the couch, so he wouldn't have to share it with any of the other two guys there with him.

All three looked around. The office was spacious; it had a large desk with its back to a huge window. There were plants here and there.

The feminine touch was definitely present in that room.


"Looks like you have friends everywhere, Colby," Bordeaux said in a rather sarcastic tone.

"I hear only cops have problems making friends," Jim said with a crooked smile.

He did not like Bordeaux but he would have to work with him, if he wanted to find his men.

"Look, smartass…." Bordeaux walked toward Jim.

Jim stood up to face him, but Bordeaux had to stop short when the door opened and a blond woman walked in.

"Oh, well, Jim … it's so good to see you."

Velma Hall greeted Jim as she walked inside the office.

She glanced at the other two men as she walked around her desk to occupy a large, executive leather chair.

She didn't bother shaking anyone's hand.

After sitting down she continued talking, "Don't tell me Amariah sent you to collect the money she lost at our bridge game last night? I'm not giving her any of her money back, you know? I won it fair and square"

She winked at Jim.

Jim sat down again, but not before giving Bordeaux a warning look; he then turned his head to talk to Velma.

"No, not at all … and how much did she lose last night?"

"Oh dear, not much more than she usually loses, every Wednesday night." The blond woman chuckled and then asked Jim, "And who are these gentlemen?"

She asked as if she had just noticed them in her office.

Bordeaux did not wait for Jim's introduction; he introduced himself and his partner. Velma did not seem impressed by the fact they were police officers.

"Well, gentlemen, since I believe a little card game among best friends is hardly considered 'gambling,' I take it that's not the main purpose of your visit here. So, how may I help you?"

Velma asked with a very polite smile.

She was a woman in her early sixties and wore more makeup than perhaps she should have, yet her natural -and delightful- charm was her real asset.

"We are here on a police investigation, Mrs. Hall," Bordeaux stated as he watched Jim pacing in the room.

Jim walked to the window as he said, "Truth is, Velma, we need your help."

◆

Andrew was always eager to start a new assignment.

He did not waste any time, after Jim left his desk, and called Chuck over the phone, to the audio room.

"Hey! Colby wants us in his office in five. What are you doing down there, anyway?"

"I was looking for a new lens for the camera … The one I have right now is scratched. Are we in trouble with Colby?" Chuck asked, somehow concerned.

"I don't think we are; not right now, anyway." Andy chuckled and continued speaking, "I think he's going to send us out on an assignment tonight, so get your butt up here, at once!"

"Okay, okay, as soon as I sign the forms for the new lens."

"Chuck … get your ass up here right now," Andy almost ordered.

"Damn it, Andrew ... I'll be right up."

Jim Colby drank his coffee slowly as he stared at the piece of paper in his hand.

He kept replaying in his head the conversation he had heard, only minutes before.

Maybe those two were talking in code. Perhaps it might be mobsters, arranging a hit ... Maybe they have someone down in the basement and want to 'dispose' of him ... or maybe this was a ghost investigation.

A hunted mansion is not something unheard of.

Mrs. Fennigan said the maids were terrified to go down there ... What was 'down there,' anyway?

Whatever that might be, was 'big' and 'made horrible sounds.' That was for sure.

*It also needed to be 'disposed' of.*

The door flew open and the two men in charge of the night shift news investigation showed up.

"Sorry, Mr. Colby ... Jim! Sorry for the delay.... We're here now," Andy said as he pushed Chuck inside the office and closed the door behind him, with a nervous smile on his face.

"Oh ... yes, good. Sit down, boys. Listen, I have something here. Some information that might be interesting to broadcast live tonight; I need you guys to go to this address ... er... I need this piece of paper. Write the address down in your own notebook, Andrew."

"Do you know what kind of assignment this is? What are we looking for?"

Andy asked as he copied the address into his pocket book.

"I'm not quite sure ... Something is going to happen at a party Mr. and Mrs. Fennigan are throwing tonight. The Major and Governor will be there; so, worst-case scenario, you guys will be covering a social and political event ... I think."

"How strange. I thought the Major was still in bed after yesterday's gall bladder surgery … Brad from the morning news covered that story yesterday," Chuck said.

Chuck received a blank stare from both men; he felt a little uncomfortable.

"Oh … well," Colby kept going, "maybe he might not be attending the party tonight, but the point is this: I want full coverage of what happens in that house … Don't focus too much on the party; there's something in the cellar that might be of public interest. Try to talk to the maids or the butler or even the yardman –if there is one; just get inside information on the people who live there. Find out what they do, who they are … anything. We will stay in direct contact once you guys get there, and if the story is good I'll get you live tonight, during the news broadcast. This is a very important assignment, boys. You hear me?"

Chuck and Andy nodded.

"Okay, men; so get your asses on the road, make contact with Bryan at the main cabin when you get there, and show me some images as soon as you get there. I'll decide if I send you live to air or not … Now, get going."

As they rode in the small TV news car, Andrew and Chuck had a conversation.

"I am not quite sure about this one, Andrew," Chuck said.

"Why? It's just another weird assignment on the night shift … Nothing special about it."

Andy tried to joke a little; but all in all, he felt as uneasy as his partner did about the whole thing.

"Am I being paranoid or did you see Colby being all weird about this?" Chuck insisted.

"Yeah, you are one paranoid crazy motherfucker, Chuck. You almost blew it with your lens issue."

Andy let some steam out, while looking out the window.

Chuck was driving.

"Hey, knock it off! If I hadn't had this 'lens issue,' we would have aired live tonight with a scratched lens; now THAT can put us on the street, you know?"

Chuck said in his own defense.

He looked at Andy for a second and then concentrated back on the road.

"So, in your opinion, Chuck, what's so 'weird' about this assignment?"

Andy went back to the original topic, without even knowing why he was so upset. Maybe the stress of the past few days -without a good story to cover- was finally taking its toll on both men.

"I don't know. We don't have enough intel, to begin with. Then, well … Colby, there was something about him. I wonder how he came across this tip," Chuck said, wondering more to himself than to Andy.

"Oh, Chuck … c'mon. He's a very professional journalist. Have you heard about the 'never reveal your source' statement? Well, I didn't care to ask him anyway. In case you haven't noticed, Chuck … the last time we aired was about five days ago, with the insurance fraud case. I haven't been able to come up with any other material to cover our asses in the past week. And besides, if Colby asks us to interview Satan himself, we will … There! Turn left at the oak tree; we're almost there, if this is the right address."

Andy said as he tried to read notes from his pocket book, in the dim light of a lamppost they just passed.

"Interview Satan himself," Chuck imitated Andy with a clenched jaw, and then turned to his friend to say, "Who's the crazy motherfucker now?"

◆

Velma looked at her computer screen and said, "This is very strange … There was one phone call made to the TV station around the time you say, Jim. However."

"What is it, Mrs. Hall?"

Lt. Bordeaux asked, walking closer to her desk.

Maybe he could take a quick peek at the screen. It was not like him to remain passive during a police investigation; no sir, he needed to start calling the shots around there.

Jim was by the window, and felt apprehensive to see Bordeaux approaching Velma's desk; Smith was sitting on the other side of the office, working hard on one of his fingernails, as usual.

It was a real mystery how Smith always found a new fingernail to bite off. One would think he had run out of, long time ago.

"Mr. Bordeaux, please … Go back to your seat. These files are confidential; I can't talk to you openly about them without a police warrant … and you don't have one right now with you … now do you?"

Velma asked, looking the officer above her eyeglasses. Like a very strict schoolteacher would regard her naughty student.

Bordeaux took a few steps back and walked away from Velma's desk as he said, "No, I sure don't have a warrant."

He felt annoyed.

Velma continued talking in her always polite voice, "Mr. Bordeaux, you must understand that if I agree to do this it is because those two boys are still missing … and because Jim is such a good friend of mine. But as CEO of this phone company my position is compromised if anyone knew what I am doing for you, right now. I hope you understand this and try to work it out with Jim. I also hope you understand that I'm not doing this for you, Mr. Bordeaux."

Lt. Bordeaux was sure she called him 'Mister' just to aggravate him. And although he did not look at Jim, he could feel the way Colby was looking at him, maybe with a smirk on his face.

Jim was certainly the teacher's pet.

Jim was not smiling all right, but he could not help thinking that would teach Bordeaux a lesson; if the officer wanted to find out something from Velma, he would have to back off.

Jim turned to Velma and said, "Can you tell us what you have on your records for last night, at the TV station? Any incoming calls to the number I gave you?"

Velma looked at Jim, and her features softened a little. She took her reading glasses off and placed them on her desk, next to a beautiful flower vase full of fresh Gardenias.

"Yes, Jim, this is going to be hard to explain but bear with me … Look, there was a phone call made to the number you gave me; for some reason the call skipped the main switchboard, altogether. That tells me this must be a direct number, separate from all the other lines you might have available to the public."

Jim nodded. Velma put her glasses back on and went to look at her computer screen.

"Okay then. So at 9:14 p.m. last night there was an incoming call all right … When I tried to track it down, the lead takes me to a closed file … as if the calling number was no longer in service. Do you follow?"

"I'm not quite sure I do, Velma," Jim replied.

"Okay, let me try this in another way. For some reason a non-working number called your station number ... But there's more to this story, and… This is very strange ... That non-working number was connected to another non-working number for almost two minutes, before your 'connection' occurred. Wow…."

Velma put her hand on her chest as if to show her shock; her face was glued to the screen at that point. She started talking to herself and typing instructions for the system to perform.

She went back and forth in the system, for a few more seconds.

"Velma, there was something rather odd about the phone call I got last night," Jim said. He looked at Bordeaux and continued, "Truth is, this is how it all started. With this one phone call."

"I knew you were not telling us the whole truth, Colby," Bordeaux snapped at Jim.

"Hush!"

Velma pointed her index finger at Bordeaux and then turned to Jim, "Were the lines 'crossed' by any chance, when you picked up, Jim?"

"Yes! They were … I was at the sound cabin when the phone rang. I was nearby and I picked it up, but before I could say a word I heard two people already talking … Can you trace those two phone calls, Velma?"

Bordeaux started taking notes in his black pocket book. Smith got up on his feet and started to pace, nervously. His hand went to his mouth.

Velma said, "Yes, dear, I can … But I warn you … these non-working numbers were stored in a file that goes way back when." Velma sighed and said, "Before or around … 1954."

Smith cussed loudly as he bit off a little more than a nail this time.

He looked around and found everyone in the room staring at him.

♦

"Are you sure this is the right address, Andy?"

Chuck asked, mortified at what he saw.

"Yes, yes it is… Will you hurry up with the camera? We should have been talking to Colby at the station by now. What the hell is this place anyway?"

Andrew could not hide his surprise, either.

"Oh, sure! Now I have to hurry up, I'm not the one who got us lost by turning 'left at the oak tree' … now was I?"

Chuck said as he hurried to get the gear from the back of the small car. He left the lights on and his door open.

"Damn, it's so dark in here … It looks like anything but a party going on. I mean, look at the grass, man … it's a mess, not to mention wild and overgrown!"

Andy said as he paced in circles and looked down at the ground, lit up by their car lights.

"Well, whaddaya know?" Chuck said as he screwed the new lens into his camera, "Maybe this is a surprise party and that's why all the damn lights in the house are also out!"

"Chuck, you're not making it easy … Whoa! What the hell is that?"

Andy jumped to one side.

"Where?" Chuck asked as he turned his camera lights on.

"There! Damn it. It's a … it's a …"

Andrew kept pointing, not far from where they stood.

"A damn snake," Chuck finished the sentence for him.

"Okay, okay. Let's calm down. This might not be the place he sent us to. Let's just call the studio, please, Chuck."

"Okay, buddy, you got it," Chuck said.

◆

Velma drank some water, and cleared her throat before speaking.

"Okay, these files from 1954 don't have the four-digit numbers that initiated the original phone call that somehow bounced into the current—modern—system we know today. Which means I need to go back some more."

She looked briefly at the men, and tried to make it easy for them to understand.

She took her glasses off to rest her eyes; she then talked to the men, "You see, as of 1955 we started using six-digit numbers in the phone industry ... Of course, fifteen years later we had to add more digits due to the rapid growth, to make a total of ten-digit numbers, the ones we use today."

Velma looked at Jim and then at Bordeaux, and continued her explanation, "The phone call that reached the TV station was originated from a four-digit line used sometime between ... hmm ... Let me go back some more; hopefully we will be able to track down the name of the user."

Velma put her glasses back on and soon she was typing her way into the complicated phone system.

Jim felt Bordeaux's eyes in the back of his head.

The only reason Jim didn't think he was going crazy, at that point of the investigation, was because it was Velma Hall herself telling the story.

Jim took an empty glass from the counter next to Velma's desk and poured fresh water; he drank some and left the glass on the nearest table he could find.

His hands were shaking a little and he did not want Bordeaux to notice. But of course, Lt. Bordeaux did notice.

"I found them! Both of them!"

Velma said very excitedly, almost triumphantly and continued talking, without looking at any of the men in particular.

"The total conversation time was … a little over six minutes … hmm …. The initiating phone call was made on October 17… 1934. The phone number belonged to a Samuel W. Fennigan. Does any of this make sense to anyone in this room? Does that ring a bell?"

Velma asked, scanning the room.

She looked at the three faces staring at her; it seemed that she was now looking for some answers herself.

"It does," Jim answered and said, "Velma, please tell me this: what was the name of the line owner in the second number… the destination number?"

Velma looked at Jim for a second; she was still in shock. If any of that made sense, then Jim would have to explain it to her, later.

She felt confused and restless; she looked at Bordeaux as if looking for an answer.

She got none. He had a stupid blank stare on his face.

Velma sighed and began to punch a few more keys. She repeated the same operation four times.

She started to feel very nervous; she either kept messing up, or she did not trust -believe- the results she got every time.

Finally, Velma sighed and said, "The number belonged to a … a Morgan Nguyen. It was a commercial line … for a business named Morgan's Pest Control."

◆

"Bryan, can you hear me?"

Andrew said, looking at the camera.

He looked to his right, and then turned again to face the camera, while pressing his earpiece to his left ear.

"Bryan!"

Andy called out to the TV station, again.

"We hear ya and see ya," Bryan replied, in a joking mood.

Bryan was the studio floor manager. Andrew heard Bryan cracking his gum, as usual.

"Well… we're here… Is Mr. Colby there?"

Andy asked, feeling uneasy.

Jim came closer to the microphone; Bryan took his empty coffee mug and mumbled something as he removed the headset from his head and walked away.

Jim Colby sat down at the now empty chair; he put Bryan's headset on as he rolled up one of his sleeves.

When he was ready, he looked at the main monitor in front of him; that's where he could see Andy.

Jim leaned forward to the mike, "So, where are you, guys? Is that the place?" Jim asked but did not wait for an answer; instead, he said, "Chuck … can chuck hear me? Chuck, pan the camera around so I can take a look."

Andy stepped back and looked around him, while the lights from the camera illuminated parts of a large house behind him.

Chuck now started to pan the camera around, and all Jim saw were bushes and night bugs flying all over, attracted by the camera lights.

Jim saw the crew's small car. The lights were still on and both doors were open. There were few trees here and there.

Chuck kept panning the camera around, and Jim finally saw Andy again, with stretched out arms.

"We're here… Jim. This is the address but it's an abandoned place … er … What do you want us to do, now?"

Jim cleared his throat before speaking.

"Are you sure that's the right address?"

"Yes, this is it. This is what I wrote down … but I was thinking that maybe this is the wrong number or the wrong street … Can we double-check the address with you?"

Andy said as he tried to straighten a piece of paper in his free hand. He was holding the mike with the other one.

Jim Colby did the same; he took out of his pants pocket the rather worn-out piece of paper, and he read the address slowly and clearly to the crew.

Bryan was back with coffee; Jim handed him his half-empty mug and sent him back to the coffee room, to fill up his mug.

"Well … it looks like there won't be a party tonight … or anytime soon. This place gives Chuck the creeps," Andrew said, trying to joke a little.

Jim saw the camera panning up and down; that was Chuck's way of agreeing with what Andrew just said.

"Okay, boys. Let's do this: knock on the door; maybe there's someone living there or something. A caretaker maybe; just see if you can find Mrs. Fennigan."

Andrew agreed as he pushed his earpiece to hear better; he motioned to Chuck and a second later they were on the move.

Andrew talked to Jim some more as he walked toward the front door of the house.

"This is a very strange place; the next-door neighbor is about two miles from here, but man! This place is huge; there must be at least fifteen rooms, or windows that indicate rooms. It's a three-story house. As you can see, the yard has not been worked on for a very, very long time," Andy stopped and said to the camera, "Okay, here we are … I don't think the doorbell works anymore."

Andrew began knocking on the old wooden door.

"Mrs. Fennigan! Hello? Mrs. Fennigan? Anybody here? We are from the KLT TV station and would like to talk to you for a few moments. Mrs. Fennigan…? We hear you are having a party tonight. Would you like to comment on it? Hello?"

Andrew tried the doorknob but it seemed locked.

He then turned to look at the camera and walked away a little from the door as he told Jim, "Maybe this is a waste of time; this door is locked. I don't think anyone lives here at all, Mr. Colby … er … Jim. Is there another assignment we could cover tonight, instead?"

Jim was now drinking his fresh coffee and didn't even bother to give Bryan his seat back; instead, he kept talking to his crew, "Yeah, I agree. It's a shame; it seemed like a good lead," Jim said, leaning over the microphone.

At that point the camera jumped a little at the same time Andrew turned around, to face the door.

Andrew walked back to the door as he said in a rather excited voice, "Jim! I heard something… I think someone opened the door... Yes! The door is now open… Mrs. Fennigan? Hello? Hello?"

Andy called out as he pushed the heavy door open.

Jim felt anxious at that point. Andrew turned around to the camera and asked for permission to go in; Jim hesitated for a second or two.

He finally told them to go in.

"Mrs. Fennigan? Anyone in the house?"

Andrew called as he got lost from view for a second in the darkness of the room; it was as if he had just entered a black hole.

Chuck followed him, camera on his shoulder, and Jim and the rest of the town were about to become witnesses to a horrific story.

# The Nightshift

Jim and the crew at the TV studio watched—in sheer amazement—the interior of the Fennigan Mansion. It was like a paradisiac dream from another era.

The place was extremely luxurious; there were fine, colorful vases - full of exuberant fresh flowers- on pedestals and tables. Each vase had a different flower theme, not two vases had the same kind of flowers.

 A huge, silver and gold chandelier hung from the tall ceiling with hundreds of diamond-shaped crystals all around it, reflecting Chuck's light everywhere on walls, floors and ceilings.

There were smaller versions of that same chandelier on the interior walls as candleholders, across long corridors; and also as exquisite wall lamps that led the way to the house's interior.

Tempting visitors to want to see more, experience more.

Chuck motioned the camera to light up the ceiling; it was completely covered with colorful stories stamped in frescos: cherubs with small wings holding harps, flutes, and other musical instruments; white, fluffy clouds all surrounded the chubby cherubs.

While colorful, exotic birds of long plumage flew around, on a bright blue sky.

"Oh, my God! Jim you have to see this! You have to look at this!"

Andrew yelled to the camera in amusement and excitement, "God! Look at this vase; it must be very expensive … Hand-made in Italy, wow…."

Andrew put the vase in front of the camera to show the artisan's original signature on it, and he then put it back in its place.

Jim talked on the mike at the same time he motioned at Bryan, who was staring at one of the monitors, with the rest of the nightshift crew.

"Okay, boys, we are going live. We are coming back from commercials now... We'll be back on air in twenty seconds... Bryan! We are not coming back to the studio for the news; let's go back to Andy and Chuck now. I think they have something there. Okay, everyone get ready... Andrew! You hear me? We are going to send you live in about fifteen seconds now... Find a good position to get started... Okay, boys, don't mess this one up. Have you found anyone there, Andy? It would be good if we could find someone there to interview."

Andrew was smiling; he held his earpiece pushed against his left ear as he talked into his mike bearing the TV station's KLT logo, "I hear noises; I'm sure there's someone around here... They know we are here, that's for sure."

Andrew turned to the left at the same time that Chuck panned the camera in that same direction, "Mrs. Fennigan? Is that you? Excuse me! Can someone give us an interview, please? Sorry we came in, but someone opened the door for us..."

Jim looked at the clock -on top of the main monitor- where he and other people were now watching closely.

Was that the same abandoned place Andy and Chuck were at before? Why would anyone have such luxury inside an abandoned house?

Were the people who lived there eccentrics of some kind, or something?

All the employees at the station were more than curious to see what was going on at the Fennigan mansion.

Jim's employees were sometimes the best way to know if a story was good to air, and tonight after that first glance at the Fennigan mansion Jim knew the whole city would love to watch it, too.

All his employees were glued to several monitors, scattered around the floor.

Jim smiled.

"Andrew! Okay, this is it, boys… in 5, 4, 3, 2 …"

Jim leaned back on Bryan's chair, as he signaled the sound assistant to cue in.

Jim looked at his young apprentice on the monitor.

Andrew Wallace was like a younger version of himself, trying to get a good start in the news business; always hyperactive, always trying to find the answers to everything, or at least a good story to report.

Jim smiled a little to himself as he saw Andy waiting for his cue.

Yes, this boy here was still a little rough around the edges, but with a couple of year's work Jim would make sure he got a permanent job in the evening news.

Jim would polish the boy; after all, he had what it took to do the job.

Andy could make a good anchor for the evening news, yes, the evening news, as always: In the night shift.

"This is Andrew Wallace with KLT, reporting live from the Fennigan mansion. Earlier this evening we received a report of a party or social event taking place tonight; we hear Major Kure and Governor White will be attending. We were delighted to find a very luxurious house in a rather rustic place… We are still trying to find the owner of this gorgeous mansion, Mrs. Fennigan… If you are watching us, anywhere in this lovely house… Mr. or Mrs. Fennigan, please come to your living room or reception hall to have a word with us."

Andy then turned to the camera and said with a smile, "Friends at home, please take a look at this place; look at these gorgeous rugs. I could swear they are made of camel hair or something like that... Look at the wallpaper and decoration with a different theme in each room... Oh, gosh, are those real spears and swords? Mr. Fennigan must be a man of the world; as you all can see, he's got a serious collection of... hunting trophies in that room over there: a real, stuffed lion; a black bear—this one seems to be a grizzly bear and it's huge. Look at those claws and fangs; they are real, I'm telling you, folks ... Wow! A whole real zebra stuffed, just like the other wild animals over here, it's like we are on a Safari in Africa here in this room... and... oh, gosh...."

Andrew moved to the corridor as if he heard something and continued talking to the camera, while moving around, "I think I saw something ... Ah, there! Excuse me... Excuse me? We are from a local TV station; can we have a word with you?"

Andy turned to the camera while walking further, inside the house.

He then turned to the camera and said, "I think the Fennigans are shy people ... but I saw someone going into that room over there, just now... Jesus Christ, look at all this luxury ... Are those real dueling pistols on the wall? It's a whole collection of them! There must be like two-hundred of them here. Okay, friends, let's keep going, Chuck, are you all right there?"

Andrew asked, looking over his shoulder as he walked down the corridor. Chuck muttered something and they kept going.

Andy turned to face the camera again and said, "Here! I think I saw someone walking into this room here ... Excuse me? Hello?"

Andrew kept going through the corridor, when he got no answer in that particular room. He kept showing the eccentric taste of his hosts; each room outdid the room before.

If such a thing was even possible.

The furniture along that corridor was oriental-style; there were tall Chinese vases along the corridor, and real-life size samurai warrior statues all along that same corridor, they seemed to stand permanent guard in place.

It was as if those brave warriors would take up running after Andy and Chuck, sharp Katanas in hand, at any moment.

No, definitely there was nothing ordinary about the house at all. Or it's contents.

"Over there. There's the staircase. If you stay with us maybe we can go upstairs and try to find our hosts, Mr. and Mrs. Fennigan… Did you hear that? Just now?"

Andy asked Chuck as he looked up into the darkness of the second floor.

By now, it was obvious the lights in the house were not working; Andrew tried the switches on the walls a couple of times. The only light they had to work with was that of Chuck's gear.

They climbed upstairs, stopping to admire -from time to time- the huge paintings, hanging on the walls and the huge vases with fresh flowers they encountered along the wide staircase, on their way up.

Every step of that staircase had some ornament of one kind or another, all in good taste. Nothing seemed to be out of place or era.

The staircase walls were covered with a deep-red velvet wallpaper, matching the expensive-looking central carpet runner.

At some point, in the middle of climbing up the staircase Chuck had to tell Andy to slow down; he could not film all the house details and furniture at once, with his camera.

Everyone at the station was glued to the monitors by then; even the security guards.

It was impossible to take one's eyes off the place, and the objects Andy would pick up -from time to time- to closely show to the camera.

Every ornament seemed to come from a different country, and a different time in history.

Jim smiled at the 'oohhs' and 'ahhhs' his employees made, upon seeing what they saw. Nothing at that house was in repetition, duplicate or boring. There were not two of the same thing, yet there were hundreds of the same theme.

The whole house was a spectacle, by its own accord and merit. That was for sure.

"Well, here we are, folks: the second floor, and still no signs of the Fennigans. And if you loved this thus far, I have to say we still have one more floor up, to visit."

Andy kept walking; he was doing a great job, Jim thought. Andrew's voice interrupted Jim's thoughts.

"Hello? Anybody home…? Well, maybe we should go… this way next… and as you can see, the place is just as gorgeous and eccentric as it was downstairs. It is absolutely beautiful. Everywhere you look there's something very original… All this items must be from other countries and brought in from exotic places or something… Gosh… Chuck, take a close-up of this full-size medieval armor … It's got the gloves, hatchet, and all. I guess I could fit in it."

At that point Bryan told Jim they needed to go to a commercial break; Jim leaned forward and told Andrew through the mike.

Andy then pushed once more his earpiece and said to the camera, "Friends and neighbors, please stay tuned while we try to find someone at this magnificent place for an interview. We have to go to commercials right now but will be right back. Stay tuned. Don't go anywhere."

And the commercials replaced Andrew's smiling face in four of the monitors Jim had in front of him; the main one still had Andrew holding his earpiece, smiling at the camera.

Those two made a good team, Jim thought. Chuck was very skilled with his camera and equipment, his 'gear' as he used to call it all the time.

"Jim? Are we off to commercials now? So, what do you think?"

Andrew asked as he looked around him.

He was excited.

"I think it's a darn good story, boy," Jim replied, and he said jokingly, "We might be charged tomorrow with trespassing but it's totally worth it; look at all that shit there. Don't you boys break anything, or it's coming out of your paycheck." Jim laughed.

He then told the boys, "The only thing is that if you guys don't find anyone soon, there will be no story. It's an awesome, crazy, eccentric place, in the middle of nowhere … so what? Having lots of money to spend it on shit like that is not a crime. If you guys don't come up with something else, another angle to that story, I might not take you back on air after the next segment, so keep looking for something, anything. If you don't find anyone on the second floor, don't bother with the third one. Try going back down, instead. Go to the cellar, the basement… I need you to try to find the wine cave … A house like that most probably has a wine cellar. I would imagine." Jim said, hoping not to raise suspicion.

Andrew kept his earpiece stuck to his left ear with one finger; he then nodded and said, "Okay, we will … What's that, Chuck?"

Andy came closer to the camera, then stepped back and said, "Oh, Chuck is saying that his battery is down to a minimum now … but he's got a spare one with him, so we should be okay for the next block. He'll then switch batteries."

"Damn, did he forget to charge the battery, again?" Jim asked, concerned.

"He says both batteries are new; he doesn't understand why this one is low, but we'll be fine. No worries, we can still deliver."

Andy tried to minimize the problem.

Bryan signaled at Jim. Jim cut Andrew short to tell him they were almost back on the air.

In five more seconds.

"And we are back." Andy began speaking at his cue, "For those who are just tuning in, we would like to say that we received reports earlier this evening about a big party being held in this place tonight, and when we showed up here we found what seemed to be an abandoned property, on the outside. But as we walked to the front door, our hostess, Mrs. Fennigan, or someone else opened the door for us, and this is what we found inside the same place," Andy said as Chuck panned around.

Andy continued talking, "Nothing but luxurious items: exotic, stuffed, very real and very wild animals. Eccentric furniture all over, very expensive vases and other exquisite ornaments and full size statues displayed everywhere … Even the walls are covered with medieval objects and handmade candelabra… I could swear that some of the paintings hanging on the walls are originals from the 1800s … And the ceilings are covered in frescos with different motifs; the one downstairs had musical cherubs and exotic birds flying all over the ceiling. And this one up here looks like…. Chuck, can you…? Yes, that's better … It seems to be…. The theme up here is either Greek gods … or something with Greek mythology. Oh, God, look at that … It's all over the ceiling … Walk over here, Chuck. Let's see where it ends … Oops … careful with the furniture. Gosh, there is something in every inch of this house. It's hard not to stumble into something with every step we take… I've never seen anything like this, not even in a museum or a movie … Ah, yes; the ceiling has a huge fresco representing a deer hunt in ancient Greece, or something like that. Do you see that? Oh, and here … Chuck, please do a close-up here on the wall…. Yes, right here. Do you see that? It seems that the shapes on the wallpaper are somehow … sticking out, as if they are an optical illusion and they now appear three-dimensional; they look like they are moving on their own. I can't quite describe it. I'm sure it's the camera's light reflection that creates such wonderful illusion. Very vivid. Ah … I hear something now; I definitely hear something now… Hello? Mrs. Fennigan? Hello? Anybody … uh … What did you say, Chuck? Oh! We have to cut transmission here due to a low bat… We sincerely apologize for any inconvenience but we will be back in a few minutes … Jim, back to the studio with you."

Andy seemed a little anxious, and disappointed.

Jim was leaning over to see better; he had never seen anything like that in his life. It was like watching a crazy move that had no storyline to it, but you just couldn't stop watching it.

The place and its eccentricity was absolutely addictive.

Not to mention delightful and intriguing.

*Who are those people?*

*Who lives like that?*

And by now, even the other security guards -the ones at the front gate- were watching closely and open-mouthed, or so, Jim was told.

There was no end to whatever Andrew and Chuck had to show at that place. It was like a crazy, lovely Wonderland, minus Alice.

Plus Andy and Chuck.

While Bryan sent viewers back to the studio for more local news, Jim kept looking at the main monitor in front of him.

The light on Andy's face was dim and going out fast. Jim lost sound, too.

He grew anxious.

Even if the boys had a low battery, it should not have gone out this fast at all, unless it was on its very last leg, Jim thought.

"Andy, what's going on? Can you hear me?" Jim called out.

There was no response.

Jim looked at his sound engineer, Adam, who signaled a negative answer as he tried different channels and frequencies.

Bryan said, "Chuck must be changing batteries now … Let's give him a minute. So, what's with the lights up there, anyway? The place is covered in gold and overflowing with crazy weird stuff, but there is no power? Really? They forgot to pay the electricity bill? That's weird and very messed up, if you ask me."

Bryan was still looking at the black monitor, waiting for the boys to turn the equipment back on.

Jim talked to himself, ignoring Bryan's comment or Adam's clicking as the tried to re-establish contact, "C'mon, c'mon, boys, come back … c'mon. Call back. What's taking so damn long?"

Jim did not really expect anyone to answer his question.

"Chuck is probably changing batteries in complete darkness; give him a minute." Adam stepped in to give a logical explanation and continued, "If anyone can switch batteries in pitch-black darkness, that's Chuck."

There was a short silence and Jim almost screamed -wile frantically pointing at the monitor, "There! I see them … Adam! There's no sound!"

Jim snapped his fingers at Adam, who put his headset back on and tried some buttons on his console -once more.

Adam changed channels and in the next minute total contact was re-established.

Andrew's face faded out for a second or two and the lights went back on in Chuck's gear.

"Andrew, what the hell's going on?"

Jim demanded to know.

"We don't know; the battery ran out, very quickly. Chuck said it should have lasted at least twenty-five more minutes … but it didn't … Hey, Jim. Look, we are in total darkness here; the only light we have is Chuck's camera. We have been hearing voices and noises all around us but no one has come to talk to us yet … I believe there is no electricity here; I have tried every switch I have seen and nothing —"

Andy was trying to get to his main point -to leave the place, and fast- but he wasn't able to say the words.

Jim interrupted him.

"Okay, I understand … Why don't you try to go to the cellar now?"

Andrew looked distressed; he was sweating and struggling to catch his breath.

He kept turning to look at the same direction -over and over again, as if hearing a repeating noise coming from the same place -somewhere in the dark, a few feet from them.

Always to his left.

"Andy…?"

Jim's voice softened some; he could see both men were somewhat nervous and even uneasy, but did not quite understand why.

Andrew looked back at the camera and seemed focused again.

He said as he held his mike in front of his face, "Yeah, I'm here … Listen, Jim, this place is somehow changing … It's hard to explain how. We are having problems with the air up here; it's somehow thicker … hmm … it's becoming hard to breathe. And the temperature seems to have dropped some, too … I don't see any vents for a central AC but I do feel cold air coming from somewhere, around here. Oh, Chuck says he feels it, too. Look, Jim, if you give us a chance we will wrap up the story as we go downstairs. It would be more professional. Just give us the cue. Oh, God! This place is so strange … I could swear the walls move. It's the wallpaper … the shapes …when the light hits the motifs, I could swear they move. I'm sorry; don't pay attention to what I just said. It's stupid. I guess I'm a little tired, that's all. All in all, this place is very impressive. Just … just let us know when we are on, and I will do the rest."

"Okay, are you sure you guys are all right…?" Jim asked, somewhat concerned.

He looked at Adam and Bryan and both men shook their shoulders in silence; no one could tell what was really going on at the Fennigan mansion.

Andrew just nodded; he didn't speak; his smile was long gone.

Chuck did not seem to be in better shape; the camera shook as he breathed heavily and the last shots had been a little sloppy. It wasn't like Chuck to do that, not at all.

Jim looked at Bryan again; Bryan shook his head as if saying, "Hey, don't look at me; it's your call, Boss."

"Hi, I'm ... My name is Andrew ... Wallace and we are live at the Fennigan mansion ... For those of you who have stayed with us for these past few minutes, we would like to let you folks know that we were unable to establish contact with the owners of the place ... or any of the guests who might have attended a party that obviously... that obviously did not take place tonight ... and ... here ... we are walking back to the staircase... so we can go down. As you can see, folks, the eccentricity of this place is astonishing, and quite magnificent ... And so is the whole environment here... Oh, Chuck, there's no staircase over this end.... Let's try the other side."

Andy turned to the camera; Chuck was about to stumble into him.

Andrew said in a rather nervous voice -knowing all too well they were transmitting live, "We need to go back this same corridor; it's got to be on the other end.... Yes, yes ... I know we came up from this very end. I know.... Oh ... sorry, folks, we are a little distracted here tonight. We have been experiencing equipment failure ... and.... Did you hear that, Chuck? Hello? Anybody home? Hello...? I think whoever lives here must be having a lot of fun with us tonight; they seem to be such pranksters. Okay, we are sorry, Mr. and Mrs. Fennigan; we should have called before coming over. Hello? Can you hear me? Ah, but since you opened the door from the inside... well, we thought. Okay, never mind. We are wrapping up this story now for you, dear friends and neighbors.... Oh, my god! Where is the staircase...? Chuck, did we pass it already? Uh ... what was that? Jim, listen: we can't find the staircase ... Can you send someone over here to find us, please...?"

Andrew said after a few moments. He seemed very disoriented and confused.

"We can't find the staircase!"

Andrew repeated, now starting to panic.

"What do you mean you can't find the staircase?" Jim demanded, "It's not that big a place; go back in your tracks, damn it! We are live here, Andrew!"

Jim spoke to the mike with clenched teeth.

Andrew tuned around and stared at the darkness, as if he had just heard something, yet again. At that moment you could see Andy's breath coming out of his nose and mouth; it seemed to be freezing in there.

Jim cussed and told Bryan to cut the signal and send it back to the studio, at once.

Transmission to folks in town was cut off; no further explanation was given.

"Andy, can you hear me? What the fuck is going on there? Stop fooling around! Andrew!"

Andrew seemed distracted, even scared, looking around him; he was not interested in the place and its decorations, anymore.

He stared blankly into the camera, which was slightly sideways.

Chuck was in bad shape, too.

Bryan said, "Jim, we are back in the studio... Our phone lines have been hammered for the last five minutes... Viewers want to know what's going on. What do we tell them?"

Jim was not listening to Bryan.

Andrew looked at the camera and said, "Jim ... It's freezing in this place. Chuck can't hold the camera much longer. We are going to turn it off ... just for a little bit ... That new battery Chuck just put in about five minutes ago is already halfway gone ... and it's so cold in here. The noises around us won't stop ... There's someone somewhere around here … laughing. It's not … not a happy laugh … I can't explain it. It's evil. They are laughing at us."

# Retirement

Marjorie struggled with Jim's fishing gear.

She had no more space in the couple's SUV to put things in; she had baked a blueberry pie for the road and had other things to eat there, too.

She did not carry as much luggage as he did, and yet she smiled, thinking that women had the bad reputation of bringing excessive luggage, everywhere they went.

It was not always so.

"Darling! Are you about ready?" Marjorie asked.

"Yes, in a minute … I'm trying to find my lucky bait … The one Billy made for me when he was ten. Do you know where is at?"

Jim yelled from the other room.

"Dear … er … you lost that bait with the last trout you tried to catch… about two years ago. Jim?"

"Ah, darn it!" Jim said.

He walked from the back of the kitchen toward his wife; he was in a full fishing outfit.

Jim said to Marjorie, "You are right, I guess I forgot. I could have sworn it was still somewhere in my fishing box … But look what I found instead … my lucky fly! The shiny one, remember this one?"

"Yes, I remember. Now, can we get going? We have been trying to get on the road for over an hour, and for one reason or another you keep us here … Let's go already. I'm eager to start our vacation!"

"Okay, okay, this fly will have to do, then … But if I don't catch anything, I'll end up buying steak for two," Jim smiled.

It was good to see him smile again.

Marjorie thought that Jim had finally put that 'Fennigan Case' -as the police and press called it-behind him.

Jim got into the SUV and began driving.

Marjorie found some music on the radio; she relaxed and rolled the window down. She wanted to feel the early morning breeze on her face; she wanted to forget the past few weeks.

Jim Colby would never forget, however.

He had been a retired man for about four months now, but he still remembered.

After four months the investigation remained open; he was told he no longer was on police watch and he could leave the city and the country, if he wished to.

After driving for an hour, he stared at the highway before him and thought about things; unsolved things, and other pending issues.

He put his hand inside his fisherman's vest pocket. He touched the uneven, rough marble stone, the same one he picked up that day at the Fennigan mansion -from the old marble bench by the front door.

The same door Andrew and Chuck went through, never to return.

He made sure he carried that marble rock with him wherever he went; that was the only thing that reminded him that the place he went to that day was real, very real.

Jim didn't want to forget about that at all.

He thought of his last day at work, two weeks after the whole 'incident' had occurred -as Bordeaux would always call it, 'the incident.'

Jim had turned his resignation in, but of course, management decided to give him a well-deserved retirement instead.

In their eyes, it was the 'honorable' thing to do.

That day he barely spoke to anyone; he asked Marla not to do the cake and the usual 'farewell party' that was customary in such cases.

Instead, he sat down in his office, took the tape out of his jacket, and watched it again, behind locked doors.

He promised himself it would be the last time he would ever watch it.

He remembered Amariah handing the tape over, when he asked for it; she did not ask anything upon giving it back, and he trusted she never saw it.

He could not believe how he had lied to Bordeaux, saying in the end he did not know where the tape -containing Andy and Chuck's ordeal- was, and Bordeaux didn't think Jim had the time to make an extra copy of it either.

Maybe Bordeaux did not believe Jim's story at all; maybe the cop gave up on him, or maybe he realized Jim didn't really know what happened that night.

Lt. Bordeaux had told Jim that a month after the boys had turned up missing, it was decided by the district attorney and the state of Pennsylvania to pour lead and concrete on the front and back doors of the Fennigan mansion -as well as all the windows.

As over the years several other people they knew of, had gone missing inside the same house.

Lt. Bordeaux said they were not sure what to do with the construction yet, but for now, sealing all entrances would keep strangers -and snoopers- from going inside that 'lethal trap' again.

The second TV crew Jim sent that night was able to record a little bit of the interior at the Fennigan mansion.

However, that material was very different from that seen and recorded by the first crew.

The place had been in total abandonment for too many years. There was no furniture at all, and old paint chunks and pieces of wallpaper hung from the walls.

Spider webs covered every corner at the ceiling where the frescos should have been.

The wooden floors had rotted a long time ago and had fallen in some places, leaving big holes; the staircase was mostly gone. It was impossible to go upstairs, anymore.

Bottom line: the inside of the place was in ruins and shambles.

When police arrived they forced Jim's second crew to come out of the house; maybe in time to save their lives, too.

Who knows?


On his last day in the job Jim fast-forwarded the tape to the last few minutes -the ones that never made it to audiences.

He watched the tape in silence.

"Andrew, stay where you are. I'm sending help over. Don't turn the camera off; this is the only way I have to make sure you guys are okay."

Jim heard his own voice, pleading in anguish.

Andrew nodded without looking at the camera; he was not holding the mike in front of him anymore. It seemed as if his arm had grown tired of holding it.

The total time elapsed from the time they got inside that house to that very moment was eighteen minutes only.

Jim frowned at the sight of his scared apprentice -visibly shaking, and as he gasped for air.

The lights went off at the Fennigan house, again.

"Bryan, call the police … and get Garret and Diane ready with another camera, to go in."

Jim heard his own voice coming from the TV monitor, and he recalled the whole event.

It was as if it was happening all over again.

"You don't mean to send another crew to… THAT?"

Bryan protested as he pointed his finger to the monitor, where Andy and Chuck had been a minute before.

"Tell Garret to establish contact with me, on their way over there," Jim ignored Bryan's comment.

Jim then remembered looking at his watch that night, they had been out of contact for over two minutes, and it seemed forever.

He called Andrew and got no response.

Jim turned to Adam.

"They have the equipment off, Jim … We can't establish contact if their camera and audio are not on. There is no signal. We will have to wait," was the only explanation Jim got from him.

"Wait for what? For God's sake! What's going on?"

Jim was frantic by then. He remembered he started pacing back and forth, as he kept an eye on the monitor that showed nothing but static.

Three more minutes went by. Jim tried to find an explanation in his mind; maybe it was a joke the boys were playing on everyone.

If that was the case, they were SO fired.

No, that was not it.

He took the piece of paper from his pants pocket -once more- and stared at it.

He tried to remember the original phone conversation; maybe something he heard held the key to getting his men out of there, or at least helping him understand.

"Jim! Jim! Hurry! They're back on … Oh, my God!"

Jim heard Adam say in total shock.

Jim ran to the mike and stopped short. He could not believe his eyes.

The light was too dim; he could hardly make out Andy's face in the dark, Andy looked very different now; he seemed transformed.

He looked sleepy, tired, cold. There were dark circles around his eyes. It was as if something -perhaps the house itself- was sucking the life out of him.

Literally.

*What the hell is that place?*

Andrew had his arms wrapped around his chest and looked away, erratically.

His mike was hanging from his hand. Chuck was in no better shape; he was having hard time keeping Andrew in frame, and he was shaking constantly.

Most impressive was when Jim saw that there was some white tiny pieces of lint or something floating all over Andy.

That stuff was also on his hair and jacket, some of it was even on his eyelashes. But what was it? There was a light drizzle of something falling down around the place… something… like snow.

It was snowing inside the house!

Impossible.

"Andrew! Goddamn it! What's going on? Talk to me! You need to get out of there! NOW!"

Jim screamed; feeling his heart in his throat. It probably was now that Jim sensed real danger, looming over those two men.

Andy seemed distracted, hearing something to his left. Trying to identify what it was he was hearing.

His teeth were chattering; the light grew dimmer and then a little brighter.

They were losing power again -and fast. Andrew looked at the camera; maybe Chuck made him look.

He placed his mike close to his face and said, "Jim … anyone, please help us. This place is … haunted … It's snowing here. We felt it as soon as we turned the camera off, and there's someone talking to us … They want us to go over there, but we're not … We won't go. Jim … I want you to look at this. I leaned on this wall here … I leaned earlier to rest a bit … God! We are so tired … Tell Mandy … I love her with all my heart. Look at this wall … Chuck, you got it? You see it, Jim? You see? It really moves. It's alive. Yeah, there's something underneath the wallpaper, it wants to come out. It's growling, too…"

Andy was moving in what seemed slow motion. His words slurring, from time to time.

Chuck tried to do a close-up but all he got was a shaking frame, out of focus.

Andy continued talking, "And look ... It's sticky and there's stuff coming off from the furniture, too. Do you see this? It's like glue … Chuck … take a close-up of my hand … I know, I know, I can't breathe either. But Jim needs to see this … It's like… like flesh… The walls are made of flesh. And do you see this snow, Jim? It's not real snow… you know? Look … It's the same fleshy material… like flesh flakes … and it's way too cold in here. Chuck is crying now. Someone or something, rather, is coming for us now… Please… no…"

"Can you hear me? Can you hear me at all …? Help ..."

Four months after the ordeal, Jim still clearly remembered it.

He would never forget, and neither would the rest of his crew and employees who were at the station, watching in horror the last scenes.

The very few employees there with Jim were crying.

Soon after Andy's cries for help, all transmission was lost.

◆　　◆　　◆

# Other books by Martha Whittington:

### MW's Tales, Volume 1:
*The Hidden Knowledge*
*A Unique Team*

### MW's Tales, Volume 2:
*6 Min, 45 Sec*
*Going Back*

### MW's Tales, Volume 3:
*White Knight, Black Knight*
*ICARUS*

### MW's Tales, Volume 4:
*Saint Death*

### MW's Tales, Volume 5:
*The Unforgiven*
*Among You*

### MW's Tales, Volume 6:
*La Légion Etrangére*

### MW's Tales, Volume 7:
*Thursday Morning*
*Iceman*

## MW's Tales, Volume 8:
*A Gifted Child*
*Sand*


# *Other titles by Martha Whittington:*


- ➢ *The Fennigan Case*
- ➢ *The Jimmy Wong Band*
- ➢ *The Witch*
- ➢ *Talking Departed*
- ➢ *Finding Henry's Journal*
- ➢ *The Storyteller & The Sleeping Prince*
- ➢ *The Heart of India*
- ➢ *A Touch without A Feel*
- ➢ *Silver Spurs*
- ➢ *Heaven Ranch*
- ➢ *Might Just Take your Life*
- ➢ *Wherever you Go*

*Some of these books are now available in Spanish, look for them!*

**Talk to me at: themonksbowl@yahoo.com**